THE MUTANTSITTERS CLUB

SJ WHITBY

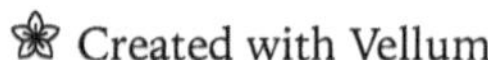 Created with Vellum

CONTENT WARNINGS

Parts of The Mutantsitters Club may be difficult for some people to read. This book contains mentions of bullying, prejudice against mutants, threats of violence, mind control, and some disturbing dream sequences. If these subjects might upset you, please take care when reading, or discuss with someone you trust.

PREVIOUSLY

Mutants! People with strange and unusual abilities—to breathe fire, or move things with their mind, or change their appearance based on their mood. They've existed for a very long time, but someone made us forget all this history. In recent years, mutants have been appearing again, springing up all over the world. Some people found their abilities disturbing and feared their powers. Then came Michael—an artificial intelligence who took over a large portion of the world and tried to destroy all mutants. That time was called the Dark Year, when anyone with strange powers kept themselves hidden because the danger was so great. In time, a ragtag group of heroes called the Cute Mutants fought against him, but the battle was difficult.

For a long time, it looked like the war could not be won.

But in secret, an ancient alien called Cybele, responsible for the creation of the original mutants, was working on a last ditch plan. She rebuilt two of the

Cute Mutants—Chatterbox and Marvellous—to be something new, a hybrid of plant and mutant. Once they were reborn and the team was reunited, together they defeated Michael. The world was restored to something like normal, but the losses were great.

Now there's a new island in the ocean, a place called Mutopia. A home built by Cybele. Mutants from all around the world have been moving there. Somewhere they can be safe.

CHAPTER ONE

THE WHOLE POINT OF NO POWERS TAG IS THAT YOU'RE NOT SUPPOSED TO USE YOUR POWERS

HAVING no powers isn't the same as being powerless. That's what my Dads tell me anyway. It's not very convincing. I know they weren't born with powers, and had to 'adjust' to their new abilities but...

"Effie! Effie, you're it!" The voice comes from a rainbow blur in the air. It's my friend Kel, who is not powerless. She has super-speed and goes all multi-coloured when she runs. We're meant to be playing *no-powers* tag but Kel gets too excited.

"Fine." I squint up at the sky as the rainbow blur descends, turning into a scruffy-looking Japanese girl with short hair, big brown eyes, and a wide smile.

She starts doing a very annoying dance, waggling her butt and twirling her fingers in the air. "Come get me!"

I stare at my feet as she dances closer, trying to look like I'm not paying any attention. Then, I strike. She's too fast, but as she skids away from me her back foot flickers with bright light.

"Cheater!" Cammie sits up from the long grass nearby. Her usual warm brown skin is still slightly green, and her long hair looks like stalks of blown grass. "Oops, sorry! Guess I'm cheating too." Her hair returns to its normal dark blonde, and the green tinge of her skin fades back to a soft brown, except for a faint reddish colour in her cheeks. "Chameleon ability is hard to turn off."

"This is why no-powers tag sucks." I hate the whiny tone in my voice, but it's hard to get rid of it. "None of you can help using your powers."

"I didn't use mine!" Dopple puffs over the lip of the hill. He's a head shorter than me, with a permanent crease in his forehead from worrying.

"You did last time," Kel points out. "I chased you and you split into four. It's not even smart, 'cause it only makes you easier to catch."

"I couldn't decide which way to go," Dopple mutters. His power is that he can make copies of him to try different choices out. They don't last very long, but if he can't decide what to eat for breakfast, he can make one version to try cereal and one to try waffles. Which is a bad example, because duh, waffles but—

"Boring!" Kel shouts. "If we're not playing tag, let's go to the beach and collect shells." She doesn't wait for an answer, just melts into rainbow light and flickers away.

"Hey!" Cammie glares after her, hands on hips.

"There's no point." I trudge after the few speckles of light that still hang in the air. It's only a handful of steps to the ridge where the whole east side of the island is laid out in front of us.

It's beautiful.

During the Dark Year, I dreamed of a place like this. Many shades of green sweep down to the sea, which is blue and grey and endless. A narrow track winds along the side of the hill to where the waves nibble at the golden sand. From here, a faint flicker of rainbow light dances up and down the beach.

"Kel," Cammie snorts as we trot in single file downwards. The sun is lowering itself slowly into the ocean, a few clouds drifting around it. The forest that crowns the top of the island stretches a few of its limbs towards us. We're not supposed to go anywhere near the trees. Not because it's unsafe, but because it's sacred. You can hear voices and meet strange figures in the forest, or so everyone says. I think they're just stories, but I've never been in to find out. There aren't many rules on Mutopia, but that's one of them.

The setting sun turns the forest shadows into little blades across the path. I avoid even these, because I'm superstitious. I dodge around each one as I jog down the hill, the slope speeding us towards the golden crescent of the beach. A series of small, colourful dinghies are dragged up high on the sand, tethered to stakes. The sand kicks up in puffs as we walk along it. It darkens towards the water until it's a deep, rich brown.

Kel has been here long enough to assemble driftwood. It spells the word *slowpokes* in large letters. She stands in the middle, waving at us. "I'm bored," she declares loudly.

"Then slow down for five seconds." Cammie's bare feet turn a delicate yellow-gold as she scuffs them through the sand. The individual grains show on her skin as she blends in without even thinking. If we stay here long enough, or she gets worried, she'll meld with the sea and sky and we won't even notice her. She gives a yelp of laughter and skips off down to the water's edge, cleaning her sandy feet in the wavelets that dance up the sand.

I turn and look up at the green sprawl of the hills. In the distance are the tiny shapes of the houses where the Founders live. My eyes follow the lines of the cliffs. Maybe they're perched up there right now, looking out over the waters. Watching us run about, looking at this incredible place they've made.

It's even more beautiful because it's safe.

Everyone calls this island Mutopia, which is short for mutant utopia. A place where people with powers can live safely. My Dads used to tell me stories at night back during the Dark Year, when we'd all sleep behind the walls. I could've been in my own room or in the trundle bed at the foot of Grandma's, but I'd rather be with them, all cramped and hot. They would whisper promises of a better world, even though nobody could imagine how to get there.

It wasn't their powers that let them dream of this future. It's just how they are.

"One day, little Effie, there will be a space carved out for us. Where we can be free and be ourselves."

They even included me, the baseline human of the family. I'm not supposed to use that word. On

Mutopia, it's considered a slur, although I've heard it plenty.

"Mutants aren't better than humans." That's something Dad Pat says a lot. So often that it's like he's trying to convince himself. He's never going to make me believe it. It's so obvious mutants are better. I was unlucky and missed out on the big genetic lottery. Blame the sore throat that kept me at Grandma's house wearing footie pajamas and eating ice cream while my Dads and my sister met an angel with a face like a rainbow.

After that, they were mutants and I wasn't. I can't cross that divide, no matter how much I try.

"We *are* different, but we're still connected," Dad Adé likes to tell me. "You can't break apart family just because some of us have changed." This part I can believe, and I like that he doesn't lie to me.

"Effie! Pay attention!" A handful of wet sand splats against the back of my neck. I spin around, but there's only a drizzle of rainbow light disappearing down the beach.

I ignore Kel, and jog across to join Cammie and Dopple in the shallow waves. The water is clear like glass, and tiny wriggling blue-green fish cast shadows on the bottom as they dart around us. The fish scatter once Dopple kicks at the water, showering both of us with cool spray. That starts a chaotic amount of splashing, which ends abruptly once Kel speeds in, sending a great wave over everyone.

"You are the *worst*," Dopple howls, standing there drenched, hair plastered to his face.

Cammie is still blinking, recovering from the shock.

Kel stands a little way up the beach, grinning. Rainbow light dances around her. She's soaked too, but of course she doesn't care. Instead, she has a cocky smile on her face, both eyebrows raised in challenge.

Even though she has superspeed, we try to chase her down.

Some minutes later, we're all lying on the wet sand, side by side in a row, with the smallest waves still lapping at us.

"I hate you." Dopple tries to wring his t-shirt out, but it clings to his body. "I don't need a duplicate to decide on that option."

Kel is still laughing. "What would you do without me?"

"Be dry?" Cammie asks.

"Be bored, more like." She flings out one arm to take Cammie's hand.

I'm starting to get cold, so I scramble to my feet, shivering a little. The sun has almost touched the horizon, making the clouds all gold and pink. It's very pretty, but I'm more focused on a line of white foam arrowing through the water towards us.

"Um." I stick my hand out to point. "What's that?"

Dopple gets up too. "It's not a shark." A duplicate appears and goes haring out of the water and up the beach.

"Fine," I say to the remaining Dopple. "One of you will survive the monster."

"Monster?" Kel waves her arms at great speed. "Don't just stand there and look at it! I can't drag you both out—I'm not strong enough! Come on! Why aren't you moving?"

The white line still moves rapidly closer.

"Because I already know who the monster is." Cammie winks at me.

"I'll leave you both to be eaten," Kel shouts.

The monster is terrifyingly close.

At the last second, a sleek head lifts out of the water. One with deep brown skin, a joyous smile, and long braids cascading down.

"Boo," she says. "Did I scare you, little sib?"

"You only scared Kel and Dopple." I grin as wide as I can. It's my big sister, Airy. We look very different because a different Dad contributed to us, but we're family all the same.

"That was amazing!" Another head pops out of the water behind my sister, followed by the rest of a tall body in a bikini. I blink and look away. This is my sister's best friend Hazel, who is... kind of intimidating and also probably the coolest person I've ever met.

"Hey, Effie." She shakes her head so that her short, rainbow-dyed hair flicks water everywhere. "I told Airy that scaring you wouldn't work. It's lucky you're the mature one in the family, or I would be very afraid for you."

Airy lies on her back in the water, soaking. Her skin glistens, and the tiny gills that run in two lines down her chest and stomach flutter open and closed. "Do we really have to get back on dry land?"

Hazel looks down, shaking her head. "Sadly, we do, or they'll send out a search party."

"What were you doing?" I ask, but they ignore me.

The Dopple who fled up the beach has vanished, the choice made to stay. Kel comes rainbowing back into view, appearing in front of Airy and holding her hand up for a high-five. All my friends think my sister is the coolest, which is kind of annoying. I mean, she's great, but not *that* great.

Airy gets to her feet. She makes a spiralling gesture in the air with her finger, and all the moisture in our clothes is sucked out. Thousands of droplets and little streams come together to form a giant ball of water in the air which drifts to hover above Kel's head. "Water fight?"

Kel is gone before the sentence is even finished.

"Ah, who would ever play tag against that girl?" Airy swipes with her hand, and the ball of water skates away to disintegrate in the sea. My sister's mutant power is to control water, which means she can throw it around as well as swim like a mermaid. She can even tow you underwater and keep a bubble of air around your head.

Cammie and Dopple gaze at Airy as if she did something magical.

It's just mutant powers, I want to shout. *You're as cool as her. I'm the only one that isn't cool.*

"Were you doing something you're not supposed to?" I ask instead.

Airy turns a lazy circle in the water and says nothing.

"There was an arrival ceremony," Hazel says. "Someone got turned away. They had Penance and Feral there, so it was serious. So yes, we shouldn't have been there." She pokes at Airy with her foot.

"People get turned away?" I ask this as casually as I can, but my heart is thumping.

"Of course." A little frown wrinkle shows in her forehead. "Didn't you know?"

"Sort of." This is a lie, but there are too many other questions crowded in behind it to say anything else. It gives me a lot to think about. About who's allowed on Mutopia, and who maybe shouldn't be there at all.

We leave the water and stop to retrieve Hazel's coat and Airy's water bottle from inside one of the dinghies. The whole time, Kel runs in circles around us. Dad Adé says her real superpower is not running out of energy.

The sea has almost swallowed the sun, and the sky is turning a blue so heavy it's almost purple. Stars pop into view, and the floating globes that mark the pathways begin to glow a gentle green. I feel very tired all of a sudden, the last one in the line as we straggle up the path leading back to town.

In the distance, something scrawls through the sky like black lightning. The mutant Penance, keeping watch, making sure nobody gets in who shouldn't. It should make me feel safe, but instead I wonder if they let me in by accident.

CHAPTER TWO

LIVING ON AN AMAZING ISLAND FULL OF WONDROUS MUTANTS IS OVERRATED

OUR HOME IS one of the cottages that the island grew. It's made of odd wooden rooms connected by leafy tunnels or giant knotholes. I like it because it reminds me of living inside the walls, like we used to. Plus it's like living inside a garden. I don't know why anyone would choose a regular home. Some kids on the island think these places are creepy because they're *alive*. But the Founders live like this too, and that means it's good enough for our little family.

We're on the edge of one of the first neighbourhoods in Emmaline, perched on the lip of a valley that overlooks a series of waterfalls that tumble down to a small, still lake. It's probably the most beautiful place in the whole world. I don't know what we did to deserve it, but I don't want to say that in case they take it back and give it to someone better.

The path from the road to our front door is lined with jasmine bushes, but overpowering even those is the smell of Dad Pat's cooking. It's his mutant power.

Three nights a week, he runs a restaurant on the island. Everyone gets their turn to eat there. You don't have to pay or make reservations—you just turn up on the night you're told. That's the way Mutopia works, for the most part. They try their best to be fair, even to someone like me.

"Finn Elizabeth and their extraordinary friends." Dad Adé beams. He's sitting on the front porch, holding a log in his hands and rubbing it gently. His power is being able to sculpt wood like it's clay, and he uses it to make the most beautiful things. He's the only one that calls me by my full name. Finn Elizabeth => F.E. => Effie.

In my family, we're given both a traditionally masculine and feminine name when we're born. At any time we like, we can choose whether we want to be seen as a boy or a girl, or neither, or both. I don't really feel like either, so I'm still Finn Elizabeth, or Effie for short because the other one is a mouthful. People use *they* to talk about me instead of he or she—like *where did Effie go? They were right here! I told them to wait.*

Airy, on the other hand, knew she was a girl almost straight away.

I don't think anyone would dare tell her otherwise, at least not on Mutopia. Our President is nonbinary like me, and one of our most famous Founders, Chatterbox, is a little bit of everything. Nobody would want to argue with them.

"We're here for dinner." Kel beams back at Dad.

"Oh, is Patty cooking?" Dad shakes his head, all mock serious, but there's a twinkle in his eyes. "With so many visitors, I would never have guessed! Where are you all when I make my famous vegetable stew?"

"Stick to what you're good at." Airy brushes a kiss across Dad's cheek and strides into the house with Hazel alongside her.

"What are you making?" Cammie crouches in front of Dad and looks at the log. "It doesn't look like anything yet."

"I'm not sure." Dad Adé's voice is low and gentle. It's the voice that always rocked me to sleep. "I have not coaxed answers from this stubborn log. She was collected from the edge of the forest, and holds her mother's secrets close."

"Drama queen," I whisper, as I place my own kiss on Dad's temple. He smells of wood and leaves, as if he's a tree himself.

"Ha! I have spoken with the mother and her children, and you do not know how stubborn they can be. Now take your friends and wash up before dinner."

Together, we enter the leafy interior of the house. It smells of chocolate and spices, all bound up with tart fruit that tickles the nostrils.

"Don't believe what the others say." Kel slings an arm around my shoulder. "We don't only like you for the food."

I know she's joking, like, at least ninety-percent know, but a part of me still feels it like a pinch on the inside of my head.

"Stop it, Kel." Cammie pokes her. "She's joking, Eff."

"I know. She doesn't have an off switch."

We head through to the bathroom, where two springs bubble up from the ground, spilling into two wooden bowls and draining away. They're fed from somewhere deep within the island by the same process that grew the houses.

Mutopia is alive. She is a gift from Cybele to all her children, including me, the scrawny adopted one. I know I shouldn't think these misery-thoughts, but they keep popping into my brain. At least I keep them to myself now. Airy tells me it's not attractive to feel sorry for myself. We all wash in the hot spring, and Kel miraculously avoids splashing anyone, mostly because she's scared of missing out on dinner. Then we file back into the main living area of the house.

Even though the house was grown, the furniture is all made by Dad Adé's hands from driftwood found on the northern beaches. It looks like it was unearthed from a fantastical shipwreck. The back of every chair around the table is different, reflecting our personalities. Dad Pat's is a steaming cauldron, Airy's is carved to look like waves, and mine is clasped hands. Dad says it's because I hold us all together. I don't know if it's true, but it's comfortable and fits me perfectly. For visitors, there's an odd assortment of chairs, but Hazel is here often enough that she has one of her own, carved with crossed pistols rising from a cloud. One of Kel's fondest wishes is to have one just for her, but Dad Adé says she cannot sit still long enough for him to keep a thought in his head.

We all take our seats. The lights that hang from the ceiling are bioluminescent plants that glow softly, filling the room. Nothing like this exists in nature, at least according to what I've learned in school. Except the mother of our island *is* nature, and she is not content with following the same recipe over and over again, just like Dad Pat.

Speaking of my other father, the curtain of vines that separates the living area from the kitchen swings open, and he stands framed in it. Everyone says I look a lot like him—sparkling blue eyes and dark brown hair that won't stay flat. Even our smiles are the same. They don't come along often, but when they do, they're surprisingly huge. I can't help but give him one of my own.

"What's for dinner?" My friends all chorus it together, and Hazel joins in.

"Something I whipped up." Dad mops his brow and hangs his tongue out like a dog. "Working frantically all day for my favourite people. Dopple, you want to help serve?"

Dopple practically throws himself out of his seat and scampers into the kitchen. The person who serves gets to clean the bowl at the end of the night, and it's a coveted spot. Dad pretends he thinks very carefully about it, but it always happens to turn out even.

Dad winks at me and disappears back through the curtain. Moments later, Dopple comes out holding a tray laden with bowls. Every single meal is made with lots of locally grown vegetables and grains. Dad's mutant power is that he can make the food taste like anything. You'd think the obvious choice is to make it all taste like cakes and ice cream, but Dad Pat is more subtle than that. He'll never tell us what's in it. People taste slightly different things, as if the magic reacts in unique ways for every person.

Tonight's dinner is hard to describe. It's savoury, or that's what I think at first. Except there's something sweet that wakes itself at the end of each mouthful, and then finishes with a taste so bright and tangy it makes my tongue tingle. Nobody speaks while they eat. It's considered rude. Pattycakes, the restaurant he runs, is the quietest place in town.

Dad Pat sits at the head of the table as he watches everyone eat. He only has a few mouthfuls, because he eats so much while he's cooking, trying taste after taste until he gets the flavours perfectly right. His eyes are bright and the corners of his mouth quirk up and down as he looks from face to face. Sometimes I wonder if he's a little bit psychic, picking up on what each person feels as they taste his creations.

As the meal finishes, the only sound is the rustling of the ceiling overhead as the wind stirs it gently. The dangling flowers which were a warm and buttery yellow at the start of the evening have faded into a cooler blue. Everyone is sated and happy.

"Perfect, my love," Dad Adé says, and his words are followed by a chain of compliments, to which Dad Pat mostly blushes and looks down at the table.

"I like cooking for people who appreciate it," he says, as if we're doing him the favour.

"Did anyone do anything interesting today?" Dad Adé asks.

"Airy took me out to the reef." Hazel smiles in the

dim light. "She made me an air bubble so we could go deeper and see all the fish that lurk there."

"So many." Airy toys with the end of one braid. "The reef is returning. Mother breathes life back into the coral, and the ocean sings brighter songs again." Her eyes glisten. "I feel it stronger every day."

"It was amazing," Hazel says. "I can't sense it the way Airy can, but it's so beautiful."

"Effie had a good day too," Kel says.

I let out a squeak. I can't help it. "I did not."

"Yes, Ms. Sefo read out your essay in front of the whole class. She said it was beautiful, and she transformed into a big pretty swaying thing while she read, which proves it was true."

It's all technically true. Ms. Sefo, who is like the nicest and best teacher you could ever ask for, gave me lots of compliments about my essay, and she *did* read it out, but…the embarrassing part is that she feels sorry for me. I'm the sad little baseline who's her charity case. And I love my friends, but she was the one who put us all together, and she's always checking up on me. The essay is only the latest thing.

Dopple blinks around. "It was really cool. It was about coming to Mutopia after the war."

Both my Dads are beaming at me, and I want to shrivel into a tiny ball. "It was okay."

"It's a lot better than okay," Kel says hotly, as if she's defending me against myself, which makes no sense at all. "Effie's super smart and knows lots of words. It felt like I was right there seeing it all."

I blink furiously at her. I don't even know where this is coming from.

"We'd love to read it," Dad Pat says.

"Me too," Hazel says. "I love all the founding of Mutopia stuff."

"You were there," Airy says. "Right in the middle of it."

It's true. Hazel's step-sib is actually Chatterbox. Yes, *the* Chatterbox. The one who saved the world with their friends and formed Mutopia. Except Hazel acts like they're just a regular person.

"Different perspectives are interesting." Hazel grins at me. "I hope you'll let me read it one day, Effie."

I don't have a single word to say about any of this, and I keep quiet for the rest of the conversation. Later, when I'm tucked up in bed in the warm dark, I finally find the courage to ask a question.

"Who's not allowed on Mutopia?"

Dad Pat makes a clicking sound with his mouth. "Mostly anyone is allowed here, but there are some rules. You have to be tolerant of mutants, of course, but also people like me and your father. Or your sister, or President Ray. Mutopia is a place of safety for people who don't always have it."

"And not only mutants." I breathe it like a secret.

"Oh, Effie." My dad's hand brushes across my forehead. "You're wanted here. You're needed."

And it's nice to hear it, but he has to say it, because he loves me.

I really hope it's true.

CHAPTER THREE

ENTER A BULLY, AND OTHER THINGS THAT GO WRONG WHEN YOU ATTEND SCHOOL

IF YOU'VE ONLY EVER BEEN to human school, you can't imagine what it's like on Mutopia. The building has a wooden frame made of tree branches all tangled together, and the walls are made of huge leaves that can be pulled aside to let the sun or the breeze in. It changes with the seasons, and flowers bloom on the inside of it in spring.

And then there are the students. Almost everyone in my class has an ability. Some of them you can't tell, like with my friends who appear perfectly human until they start fading away, or turning into a super-speedy rainbow blur, or making copies of themselves when they can't decide what the right answer to a test question is. At least Ms. Sefo doesn't let Dopple get away with that.

There are more unusual mutants, like Sting who has corrugated blue and green skin, with a little thicket of horns on her head that drip poison. Or Titania with her giant butterfly wings or Seven, who has legs that are two meters long and jointed in so many places he folds up like a concertina when he wants to sit down. All examples of the strange and mysterious mutations that have cropped up since the dawn of Mutopia. They're seemingly random, appearing all over the world, and striking people without warning.

"Mother Cybele moves in mysterious ways," Dad Adé says whenever I ask him about it.

Once you get over the novelty of sitting next to a girl who melts in the heat like ice cream, school is still about learning equations, parts of language, how genetics work—until you break it apart with mutations that nobody can explain—and history. We do history a little differently here, with particular focus on the story of mutants, but we learn the other parts too. Great nations throughout history, and their rise and fall. Against that tapestry, our island might look very small, but it has the seeds of something incredible inside it. That was the line I ended my essay on, the one that Ms. Sefo said was remarkable. Okay, so I was a little bit flattered by that.

Ms. Sefo doesn't teach everything—we have a whole variety of teachers who come in, but she's there for most subjects and is the one everyone turns to for help. It's easy to forget sometimes, with her soft smile and kind eyes, that she's one of the Founders and that her girlfriend was the most powerful mutant in the world. Her power is to transform into different forms, mostly based on her moods, but she doesn't usually do that in class.

"Are you daydreaming, Effie?" Her voice is light, but it carries.

"No," I lie.

She's not one of these teachers that will try and catch you out to prove you wrong. The arched eyebrow tells me she knows I wasn't paying attention, and the flash of smile says she knows I'll do better now. I bend my head to my tablet, and focus on completing the rest of the math quiz while Kel hums behind me.

After school, Dopple heads off to help his parents. They run a very popular general store in the middle of town, and expect as much of his assistance as possible. His mother is very good at finding ways to use his ability, so it's like she has many diligent sons. It seems mean, but he doesn't seem to mind.

Kel races off on one of her many laps of the island. Eventually, she'll wear herself out and come find me, demanding to play a game. I don't know where Cammie is. Sometimes school is a lot, with so many people, so she fades away. She always turns up eventually, materialising out of thin air wherever one of us is, as if nothing has happened. We never *say* anything about it, because nobody wants attention drawn to the little awkwardnesses we have. All of us find school hard to deal with sometimes. Maybe that's why Ms. Sefo put our study group together.

So I end up walking home on my own. I consider heading to Dopple's to scrounge candy, but his mother will most likely put *me* to work, and there's homework I should do if I'm going to avoid Ms. Sefo's raised eyebrow again. At the intersection, I turn away from the path towards town, and follow the one that curves towards home. It runs all the way along the ridge top, and there are lots of people doing various errands. The views are amazing here, the hills dotted with wild-flowers and the river snaking down to spill into the bay.

I've seen it enough times that I'm used to it. As soon as I get the chance, I take the shortcut through a little apple orchard. I skip through the trees, hoping to find some fallen fruit. I'm zigzagging my way to the far side when I hear the first laugh.

I stop dead, half-sheltered by branches and leaves. This is fine. There's no reason the laugh has anything to do with me. Except I don't really believe that. I stand and wait while my heart thumps.

There's no recurrence of the sound, so I step out into the path.

Standing at the end is a familiar figure. Not in a good way. Not in the least. The laughing kid has curly blond hair and two wings made of dazzling light. He's got a sneer on his face. The bigger problem is that if Firewing is here...

"Hello, Linus." The voice comes from behind me, and using that name means they're definitely talking to me.

I glance over my shoulder and see Deadshot. She copied her name from a comic book character, which is an automatic fail if you ask me. If you see her without her mouth moving, she's very pretty with her heart-shaped face and strawberry blonde hair. When her mouth *is* moving, it's usually insulting me, and *that's* normally a precursor to her throwing something. As you might figure out from the name, she never misses. Right now she's holding a fresh green apple in each hand, tossing them up and down.

I should have run faster when I heard the laugh.

"It's very rude, Linus." Deadshot whips one apple through the air, terrifyingly fast. It hits the trunk of the tree beside me and shatters, spraying me with little chunks of broken apple. She didn't miss. She's toying with me.

I taste sour juice on my lips. "What's rude?"

"Not to say hello when someone talks to you."

"It's not my name." I shouldn't have said that. If I make a run for it, sticking to the trees, maybe they won't catch me.

"Not your name? Did you hear that, Firewing? I was sure they were called Linus."

The boy's enormous glowing wings beat one single time. He glides half the distance towards me, the toes of his shoes brushing across the ground. "That's definitely the name I heard. Why do they call you Linus, Linus?"

Linus means baseline. It's one of the oh-so-clever names the mean kids come up with to pretend they're not saying a word that might get them in trouble. It's not fooling anyone, especially me. There's nobody else around to hear it though, and if I go and tell someone like Ms. Sefo, that will only make everything worse.

I take a step backwards until I'm pressed up against the solid trunk of a tree. If I slip around and make it across three more rows, I'll be on the other side of the orchard. From there you can see our house around the valley. Maybe that close to home, they won't do anything.

Deadshot tosses the other apple into the air. Her lips rest in a smile that's far from pretty.

"My name isn't Linus." I make a break for it.

I get through two rows of trees. There's only one more between me and possible freedom.

Then Firewing swoops down out of the blue sky and catches hold of my shoulder. There's a swooping feeling in my stomach as he lifts me, my legs flailing for the ground. Something clenches in my chest. He banks with me and dips down, dragging me down the path between the trees. It's too fast for my legs to keep up and my knees smack into the dirt painfully.

When he releases me, I sprawl on my face. There are tears in my eyes. I've bashed my lip and I taste blood. Firewing hovers, his wings like glowing signs in the sky. I scramble, trying to get to my feet, but one leg is sore and the other skids in the dirt.

Something hard hits me in the shoulder and spins me around. I clap my hand up to where it hit, but that makes it hurt worse. I'm surprised a chunk of me wasn't knocked away, like a gingerbread man with a bite taken out. Juice glistens on the blue material of my shirt.

"You don't belong here." Deadshot steps out from among the trees. There are two more apples in her hands, but I can't look away from her wide smile. "Now tell me your name."

"Their name is Effie." A new voice. A possible rescue. I look around frantically for the source.

Hazel strides out from among the trees, dressed in a long black coat. Her short hair is damp and clings to her face, the strands like multiple interlocking rainbows. "And you'll leave them alone."

"Yeah? Or what?" Deadshot turns her attention away from me, the cringing thing on the ground, and towards the new threat.

Firewing starts to ascend slowly. "Deadshot, I don't think—"

"Shut it, Fire." The sneer is back on Deadshot's face. I can hear it in her voice. "She might be wearing a badass coat, but Hazy here doesn't—"

Deadshot flings the apple at Hazel before she finishes the sentence. I barely see it move through the air.

Hazel is faster. A pistol materialises in her right hand. It's ornate, made of wood and gold. I can't read it from here, but I know that the word *Dream* is written down the side. The barrel of the gun sparks and spits a trickle of flame.

There's no sound, but the apple disintegrates as if it had never existed. For a moment, an afterimage hangs in the air—a towering tree laden down with fruit.

"The seed dreams of the tree it could become," Hazel says.

"There's more where that came from." Deadshot clutches her other apple tight.

"And I have another weapon." Hazel holds out her empty left hand. Her fingers twitch. The pistol that appears is identical in shape to Dream, although it's black and silver as if it's been woven from smoke and moonlight. There's a word written on its barrel too, although it's in an even deeper black, nearly impossible to read. *Nightmare.* "Would you like me to fire it?"

"You wouldn't." The sneer in Deadshot's voice is a ghost of what it once was.

"I'm not a fan of bullies," Hazel says.

Firewing is smart enough to know when he's beaten. He flaps his glowing wings and spirals frantically upwards.

Hazel doesn't even look. She simply moves her arm to point overhead and fires. A streak of black smoke erupts from the barrel of the gun. It smells like an extinguished match, and flies straight for Firewing. I don't think there's any evasive action he could take to avoid it.

It pierces his heart neatly, but he doesn't stop. In seconds, he's out of sight.

"Missed." Deadshot smirks.

"Tell me that tomorrow." Hazel points Nightmare at Deadshot. "As I said, I'm not a fan of bullies. I especially don't like people who push Effie around. They're a sweet kid. And even if they weren't..." She sighs, and pulls the trigger. Another flicker of black light flashes from the barrel of the gun and wreathes itself around Deadshot. It's only visible for a moment or two, then it's gone, as if it was an illusion. "Some say I should only fire my gun in the defence of mutantkind, but I call this exactly that."

"You..." Deadshot's shoulder's slump and the other

apple falls from her slack hand onto the ground. She turns to face me, but the sneer is gone from her face and her eyes are empty. "I need to go home." She shuffles back through the lines of trees and is gone.

The guns evaporate from Hazel's hands, leaving them empty. "Don't worry, Eff. I only gave them little dreams. But maybe they'll think twice next time." She crosses to me and holds out her hand. "Let's get you home and cleaned up."

CHAPTER FOUR

IN WHICH MY FAMILY TAKE CARE OF ME, AND I'M A BAD PATIENT

WE GET BACK to my house, but nobody's home. Hazel still walks in as if she owns the place.

"Lie down over there." She directs me to one of the mossy couches, which I collapse into. I'm starting to realise how many different parts of me hurt. Hazel fetches warm water and a cloth and begins to clean my face. Every time she touches me, it stings.

"I'm fine," I tell her, over and over, but she doesn't listen.

"You're not, and you don't have to be. Sometimes you remind me of your sister, blatantly denying the obvious." Her face is concentrated as she dabs at me. "Has that happened before?"

"No," I say, and watch her brows draw down. "Sometimes. Never that bad though."

"Do they call you that often?"

"What? Linus?" I want to turn away from her, but she's still cleaning the dirt from my legs. "Why wouldn't they? How is it untrue?"

"They shouldn't try to make you feel lesser because of it. My mother is human, same as both my siblings *and* my step-parent. That makes me quite a fan of humans. Besides, I was one myself up until quite recently."

"Oh."

"You're far from the only human on this island, you know. It might not feel like it sometimes, but they're there." Her lips press into a thin line. "I'll have a talk with Dylan about it. I know they're worried about anti-human prejudice. I suppose it's inevitable, given we're a haven for mutants, but there's no need to make our own hatred."

Her voice is very soothing, and it helps to distract me from the pain of her prodding me and cleaning my scrapes. The most sore part is my shoulder where Deadshot hit me with the apple.

I don't spend a lot of time thinking about the other humans. Most of them arrive here in the company of mutant parents or siblings or children. It's better than splitting their families up based on mutant and human lines. Despite this, I always assume *everyone* here is a mutant, hiding some fabulous secret beneath their skin, but maybe some are ordinary like me.

"What the—?" Airy stands in the doorway, a scowl on her face. Her deep brown eyes are usually full of laughter, but right now they contain storms. "Who did this?" She crosses to my side in a handful of strides.

I stare at the mossy back of the couch, but Hazel answers for me.

"A couple of kids from school."

"I'm going to—"

"They're going to sleep badly tonight." The corner of Hazel's mouth twitches. "I came to the rescue."

"Like a badass," Airy snorts and then crouches beside me. "You okay, kiddo?" She brushes one knuckle down the side of my cheek. "Do I need to follow up and make sure they've learned their lesson?"

"No." I close my eyes against the humiliation. "I want everyone to forget about it."

"Who was it?" Airy asks Hazel.

"The kid with glowing wings and the Hawkeye-type one. She threw an apple at me, too."

"I'll take her for a swim," Airy glowers. "Teach her to mess with my sib *and* my bestie."

"I took care of it already. If you want to be helpful, fetch me the first aid kit so I can patch up the worst of these scrapes."

Airy stomps off, muttering words far worse than baseline under her breath.

By the time Hazel's finished patching me up, my Dads are home. They both rush to my side and give me very careful hugs before demanding to know what happened. I spill the story in halting words.

"Thank you, Hazel." Dad Pat's voice is shaky when I'm done. "I'm glad you got there when you did."

"I wish it had been earlier." Hazel pulls her coat around herself tightly and shivers. "It's lucky I came that way at all. Usually I don't, but I was running late and... Poor kid."

I've been feeling super grateful towards her, but some of it evaporates when she calls me *poor kid*. I'm only four years younger than her eighteen after all. It's not like I'm a baby.

"I'm actually fine." I swing my legs off the couch and get to my feet. I only wobble a little bit. "It's not much worse than a fall."

"It's still scary." Dad Adé puts an arm around my shoulder. "I'll talk to the school tomorrow."

"Talk to the school about what?"

"The bullying situation. It's unacceptable. Those children need to understand that—"

"I understand why they do it," I blurt. "I remember being out on the streets buying food because you couldn't go out safely. The soldiers stopping people and giving them the gene tests. I saw people being taken away in vans. Both Deadshot's parents got taken and she doesn't even know where they went! Everyone made a big deal about how Ms. Sefo read my essay out in class, but she couldn't even read Deadshot's! When she tried, she transformed into a scribbled outline of a person, half-melted with tears."

There's a lot more I could say, but I've cried enough in front of Hazel. Everyone calls it the Dark Year, but it was more like a creeping nightmare. The world changed in little snippets until you couldn't recognise it anymore. Mutants like my family had to hide from the great golden eyes of Michael, the AI who controlled everything and saw too much. I was the only one who was safe to go out into the world.

Hazel lets out a long sigh. "Now I feel bad for giving her a nightmare. God knows what the poor kid will dream about. I just got so mad seeing Effie pushed down in the dirt."

"What Deadshot did is still not okay." Dad Pat's voice still shakes. "We don't want to replicate suffering and prejudice here. I love that you're compassionate, Effie, even towards someone who hurt you."

"I'm still going to talk to Ms. Sefo," Dad Adé says. "She'll know the best way to deal with this. And Effie, I hope you know that there's nothing wrong with being human. You're not responsible for what happened to Deadshot or her parents, and what you did for our family during the Dark Year was—"

"I know." I don't need to hear about how brave it was all over again, because I was one of the lucky ones. Even when it got bad, my humanity kept me safe. All the lies I told, shopping at five different places in the city, learning all the safest routes home—it was to protect the real people in danger. My family.

"And you don't deserve to be treated that way." Dad Adé's eyes are worried.

"I know that too." It doesn't make me feel any better because it's unsolvable. Humans did a lot of terrible things to mutants. I know I'm not responsible, but I might be the closest one that Deadshot can lash out at. Getting hit by an apple and going face down in the dirt isn't fun, but it's something I'll heal from.

DINNER THAT NIGHT is much quieter. The restaurant that Dad Pat runs in the town is open, but he's been busy reorganising bookings because people don't have babysitters. He offers to cancel the whole sitting, but I insist he goes. People deserve their turn. He actually listens to me, although he does whip me up something special first. It's one of my favourites from when I was a little kid, that lurches from mouth-twistingly sour to deliciously sweet and back again like a rollercoaster of flavour.

Dad Adé only has a few bites before pronouncing it inedible, like he always does, and he laughs his deep, reassuring laugh every time my face screws up. After dinner, we sit on the porch and he works on his mysterious log again. His hands trace the grain, as if he's reading a message written along the surface.

"Is that really from the forest?" I ask. "Like *the* forest." I'm referring to the most sacred part, that nobody is supposed to go into, at the very peak of the island. It's not an official law. Kids sneak in on dares, but I don't know of anyone who's been in there *twice*. The stories say that if you try to enter, you'll magically appear on the other side, or find yourself sent somewhere else. I've always been too scared to try.

"The Crown, yes." Dad turns the wood over in his hands. "I didn't go in there. I was walking along the path when it rolled out in front of me. An obvious gift."

"But the wood isn't telling you what it wants to be?" I frown. The wood is usually so eloquent for Dad.

"No, she is, but I am trying to convince her otherwise. She wishes to be a pair of weapons for a pair of wielders. I do not like weapons, and so I am wondering whether she can be gently persuaded." He laughs as his long fingers curl around one end of the log. "No, she is predictably stubborn. It seems I cannot fight the inevitable. They will be beautiful weapons indeed, and at least they will be in the care of two I trust."

"You mean...?" I can barely bring themselves to say their names. "Biome?"

Chatterbox and Marvellous are—or were, the stories are confusing—two mutants who died on an island very like this one and were reborn as something new. They are both plant and mutant, creatures made by Cybele herself, the spirit that lurks at the center of the world. Together they are known as Biome. This island was created for them, or by them. The stories are confusing, but they're real. I've seen them. A few weeks ago, Chatterbox even spoke to me and saved me from Firewing stealing my bag again. I acted super embarrassing and called myself a baseline right in front of them. They were completely nice and normal, and didn't seem like a magical plant person at all, except for the fact they were slightly green and wreathed in flowers.

"Yes." Dad smiles. "These will be for Chatterbox and Marvellous. Gifts from the mother for her most terrifying and ferocious children." He winks at me. "They are kind, but they are also deadly."

I give a little shudder. It's like having gods walk among us. Strange old gods like the ones from myths, creatures we don't fully understand. One day they might appear perfectly charming and normal, the next they might be fighting dark monsters that threaten our world.

"Don't worry, Finn Elizabeth," he says. "They are our protectors and we have nothing to fear from them. Our enemies, on the other hand..."

Under his gentle coaxing, the wood softens and melts away, drifting in dancing curls of liquid to the ground, where they form shapes like letters in a language I don't know. The tip of a blade begins to form at the end of the log, narrow and wickedly sharp.

CHAPTER FIVE

NOTHING BAD COULD POSSIBLY HAPPEN WHEN YOU SNEAK OUT OF YOUR ROOM AT NIGHT TO VISIT A SCARY FOREST, RIGHT?

DAD BUNDLES me off to bed early, but I can't sleep. It's not because I'm sore, even though I am. My brain keeps bouncing between remembering Deadshot's sneer and what Dad said about finding the log in the forest. The mother, giving him a gift and a task. A message from a being too powerful to understand, who reaches out to drop something in his path.

What it means is people can communicate with her. Biome might have a direct line, but she holds out her hand to others too. And *that* means I might be able to reach back. Everyone says that Cybele works in her own time, but I'm tired of waiting. I don't want to be a baseline anymore. Sometimes you need to ask for things. Demand them, if you want them badly enough. And I do want this. I think. I need to go out into the wild world on a quest, and plead to become something else. Something that *belongs*.

The house is quiet. Despite the walls being woven leaves and reeds, they absorb the wind and make it perfectly peaceful. Even the roof barely ripples. I pause outside my room and listen. From next door, I can hear Airy breathing, heavy with sleep. I slip out of my own bed and into the hallway. There are still no other sounds, so I pad past by Airy's door, my bare feet silent on the smooth wooden floor.

The real risk is Dad Adé, who sometimes gets lost in his work and stays up for hours and hours. I creep through the living area without any sign or sound of him. The front door opens noiselessly and I poke my head out. High above, the moon is almost full and soaks the porch and the path in pale light. The log lies unattended on the porch, twin blades jutting from the end. Each is equally long and sharp with a delicate twist halfway up. They're beautiful and for a moment I think about touching them to see how sharp they are. No, stabbing myself would not be a good start. I do wonder about shedding blood though. Old stories about gods often involve blood.

I jog down to the end of the path. The night air is cool, with a little breeze, but not so much that I need a jacket. When I stop and look over my shoulder, the house looks ghostly. The moonlight clings to the leaves, and it looks as if it's crawled through a crack in the world to appear here. I turn my gaze to the road that glows faintly as it winds around the valley.

"Miles to go," I whisper.

I've never been out in the night alone before. Something about it makes me want to run. I know it's safe. I know nothing is chasing me, but I hurtle along as if there is. Even though my feet are bare, there's nothing to hurt me or make me stumble. Everyone says that Cybele takes care of her people on the island. I hope that's true even for me.

Once I'm around the valley, I avoid the scene of my humiliation and strike out across the fields that lie between me and the darker shadow of the forest. Further towards the coast, these fields are full of crops tended by the handful of mutants whose abilities mean we easily grow enough food for all our needs. One day, if the population of the island keeps growing, we'll need all these fields. Right now, these ones are only full of long grass, slightly damp with dew.

The moon is almost directly overhead and her pitted face shines down as I arrow towards the forest. It lights me like a spotlight, and I wonder if Farsight in her tower turns her gaze towards me. Will she care about one small rogue human loose in the night, or is her attention on protecting our shores and the dangers in the human world?

Let's hope she's preoccupied, because I'm nearly at my destination. From this angle, the trees look much taller. The foliage tangles together, swallowing most of the moonlight, except where the light filters down to make a faint path.

I take it as a sign of welcome.

It's warmer among the trees, as if the tall pillars of the trunks are heated. I brush my fingers across the rough wood, but there's no warmth. High above, the foliage meshes together in a wild tangle, the few wind-tossed gaps making the path flicker but not fade. I'm not at the Crown yet, but the path only heads in one direction.

"Hello? Mother Cybele?" My voice gets lost in the deep silence of the forest, like a pebble dropped in an enormous lake. "I want a gift."

There's no answer. All I can do is follow the path, stumbling deeper and deeper. The foliage gets thicker, and the trunks get closer together. They look more gnarled, as if they've been standing for hundreds of years. The island is barely a year old, so they can't be. Then again, I *am* out in the night hoping for a gift from something impossible.

"Mother Cybele." I pause in a small spill of moonlight barely large enough for me to fit in. The next lit up area is a few paces to my left. I think they're getting further apart.

There's a flicker of movement off to my right.

I spin to look, but there's nothing but trees. "Hello." My voice shakes. "Show yourself, please."

In all the stories, quests are never easy. You need to prove yourself. The quests I used to go on were so mundane—reach the pharmacy without drawing attention. Order medicine without shaking. Face the soldier patrols without fear. Lie in the face of authority. Don't give away your fathers and sister hiding in the walls of your grandmother's house. Keep your secrets folded close. Don't even let them see a whisper of it in your eyes or on your tongue. Let them take your blood, over and over, without flinching, and watch the test result glow green. Be the baseline human that allows your family to live.

I don't need to be that person anymore.

"Please." I take quick steps to the next pool of moonlight. "I want one favour. You've given it to so many."

Another movement rustles nearby. Something's watching me.

I cling for the nearest tree and let out a squeak. "Who's there?"

Most of the stories I've heard of the forest are from Kel. She talks about plant zombies, monstrous creatures that are failed attempts at building new versions of Chatterbox and Marvellous. They apparently patrol the forest, murdering the unwary and using them as fertiliser for weird and wonderful gardens.

Gardens like the one I can see at the edge of the next patch of moonlight, thronged with flowers that are either deathly pale or the rich red of blood.

It's only a Kel story. She's never been to the Crown.

I'm pretty sure she's making it up.

Except there are the flowers.

And now a pair of eyes looking at me. They're large and faintly luminous gold. They blink again. I'm so scared that I can't even squeak.

Something twitches in the darkness, and a sob finally bursts from my throat.

"Mother," I gasp. "Help!"

"Aw, kid. It's fine. Sorry for the fright." A woman steps into the patch of moonlight. She has very short fur all over every patch of exposed skin in rippling patterns of brown and gold. A long tail, tipped with a sharp metal spike, twitches at her shoulder. She's smiling, but it's not very reassuring because her mouth is crammed full of very sharp shark teeth aside from two very long canines. All up, she's an unmistakable figure.

"You're," I gurgle. "You're."

"I'm." She grins at me and I try to stop shaking. "I'm Feral."

"Bodyguard to Biome," I blurt. "You're practically their sister. And you're one of the Founders!"

"My reputation precedes me." Feral laughs. "Or gossip, at least. And my days of scaring scrawny kids in the forest should be long past." She leans against one trunk. "I *am* curious about why you're here."

I stare at the ground. "I need a favour. The mother gave my Dad Adé a request and I thought..."

"You could make a deal." Feral blinks solemnly. "No powers, right?"

I nod.

"Look, I get it." Feral holds her hand out, as if she wants to soothe me. "It's got to be tough, living here and hanging out with all these powered kids. But calling Cy like that isn't a good idea."

"She's the mother of mutants, isn't she?"

Feral scratches her head, pursing her lips thoughtfully before she speaks. "Mother's not a helpful word. I get why people use it, but you wouldn't ask a wildfire or a tornado for a gift."

I think she's trying to be kind, but all I can hear is *no*, which is hard to take from an actual superhero with a mouth full of vicious teeth. "But she might give me *something*," I say stubbornly. "And sometimes things are still standing after a tornado."

Feral gives a strange yelp of laughter that sounds like it has a purr threaded through it. "Very true. But you look like you've been in the path of a small tornado already. Might be enough excitement for one day, huh?"

Some of the fur around her neck is standing on end. Is she actually scared? Her ears twitch slightly and she holds out her hand again.

"What's your name, kid?"

"Effie."

"Okay, Effie. I think we're done here. Jump aboard and we'll make our escape, shall we?"

My eyes are nearly as wide as Feral's. "Escape from what?"

"Wildfire, tornado, terrifyingly powerful energy being neither of us are equipped to deal with? Take your pick."

"No." I grit my teeth and wish I could dig my feet into the soil. "I'm going to ask the mother for a—"

A beautiful woman with dark green skin steps out of the darkness. Her body is woven around with vines and white flowers dot her brow. She moves like the wind in the trees, rustling and unpredictable. Her face is perfectly smooth and the perfection of it is unsettling. It puts me in mind of flowers that look beautiful in order to attract prey.

Feral says a very impolite word.

My desperation for a gift is swallowed up by a much deeper and more insistent fear. Feral is right. We should have run.

"Someone is caterwauling," the woman says. "Is that you, sweet Fairy?"

"I didn't hear anything." Feral bares all her teeth.

"It was me." I shove all the fear down, the way I used to in the Dark Year, face to face with soldiers or worse. "I came here for a gift. I need powers."

I don't even blink and she's right in front of me. Cybele. The spirit of the earth. It's not her, really. Like how you only ever see the tip of an iceberg, this is the tiniest fraction of the mother. She smells of freshly dug soil and heavily perfumed flowers.

"Powers." One hand reaches out and takes hold of my throat.

"Cy, do I need to call Biome?" Feral has one furry hand wrapped around Cybele's arm.

"Hush, my dear. I shall not hurt the stripling." Cybele tilts her head, the flowers at her brow glowing white in the light of the moon. "And nor shall I grant them powers. They are a flux, like my sweet Dylan, yet in this case it suits me to leave them untampered with. Call it whimsy, or call it the subtle twists of my plan. Either way, you shall stay the same, little one."

She leans forward and presses cool green lips to my forehead.

I black out instantly.

CHAPTER SIX

THERE'S NO WAY A PRANK LIKE THIS COULD GO WRONG

I WAKE in my bed as if nothing happened. I'd have sworn last night was a dream, except dirt and leaves cake my feet. And I can still feel the imprint of Cybele's lips on my forehead like a brand. I run through to the bathroom to look in the mirror, but there's only a smudge of dirt on my skin that's easily brushed away.

Did Feral bring me home? I consider asking my Dads, but that would involve explaining things. It feels like a small betrayal to ask for powers when they're always trying to prove to me that I'm good enough without. Plus it's extra embarrassing that I met Cybele and she said no. I'm not good enough to be a mutant. I heard it directly from the lips of the being who creates them. I close my eyes against a sudden rush of tears. I can't tell anyone about this, and somehow I need to stop Feral from telling anyone too. What if she tells Chatterbox? The most famous mutant on the planet, knowing that I'm the worst.

Right now, I have to worry about the fact I overslept

and am late for school. I run most of the way there, but I feel weirdly light-headed. Maybe it's that I was kissed on the forehead by a god. Part of me desperately wants to tell Kel this story, but the ending is way too disappointing.

Unfortunately, embarrassment is impossible to avoid. When I get to school, I discover everyone already knows about what happened with Deadshot. I have no idea *how*. Airy and Hazel don't even go to school, and nobody else was there except—

"Firewing," Kel tells me. "He was here first thing, telling everyone who'd listen that Hazel shot him with a nightmare pistol. Apparently he reported it, but Dragon blew smoke in his face and asked him what the bleep he did to bleeping deserve it."

"He spoke to Dragon?" Dopple asks. "That seems… unwise."

"Yeah, he says people can't go around shooting people with nightmares, so I said to *him* that he can't go around snatching people with his nasty claws."

"What about Deadshot?" I ask.

They all turn to look at me. "What does Deadshot have to do with it?"

"She was there! Throwing apples at us." I tug down my t-shirt and show the bruise on my shoulder. Everyone oohs and aahs over it, until Kel pokes it, because of course she does.

"She's been awfully quiet." Kel narrows her eyes and glares over at Deadshot, sitting in the corner with her friend Snake, who has a forked tongue that's pretty damn poisonous. "I think she's trying to get away without her rightful payment."

"Hazel shot her with a nightmare," I point out.

"So? That was Hazel's revenge. This is ours. You don't mess with our friend."

"She only threw an apple." I flush red at this, because I've just shown them the bruise, and everyone knows that Deadshot never *just throws* something. "And besides, you heard that bit of her essay. She's got reasons to hate humans."

Kel snorts so loudly I almost jump. "I saw a lot worse than Deadshot, and I'm not horrible to every human I ever meet. And look what happened to Cammie's brother."

I turn to Cammie, because I didn't even know she had a brother.

"He died." Her voice is very faint, as if it's fading into the background like she does. "I saw it on TV. He was fighting with the Cute Mutants, during the battle with Abigail Tanner."

My jaw is hanging down. I know this. We studied it in school. It's one of the pivotal moments in the formation of Mutopia—the point at which the Cute Mutants declared themselves a nation and species.

"Leapfrog," I say. "Your brother was Jackson Phelps."

She nods, but she's almost blended into the pale cream of the wall, so I barely notice.

"I'm really sorry."

"It wasn't your fault. It's not like you were there, is it? But Kel is right. A lot of us have suffered at the hands of humans, and we don't all take it out on you. Deadshot needs to be taught a lesson."

"I think Hazel already did." I'm weakening and they can both sense it.

"No." Cammie shakes her head firmly. "We need to. *You* need to, Effie."

"So what do we do?" I ask.

Everyone looks at Kel, but it's Dopple who speaks up first. "You know, she always comes to my family's store after school."

"I THOUGHT I told you to stack in aisle five?" We can hear Dopple's mother shouting at him from the other end of the store. It's how she triggers his powers and ends up with two or three copies of her son busily stacking until the effect wears off. She gets a lot of work out of one boy, that's for sure. The shop is mostly quiet, aside from a mum pushing around a trolley with three little kids hanging off it, each whining at a different pitch.

Kel and I offered to help Dopple, like we always do, but it's always waved away. Instead, we're perched on stools at the milkshake bar, sharing an enormous chocolate shake and working our way through a bag of donut holes. The division of labor is unfair, but we're not arguing about it.

The shop doorbell rings and Dopple lets out an enormous fake sneeze.

"Showtime." Kel grins at me and is gone in a blur of rainbow light.

I slide off my seat and head down one of the aisles. I'm not really involved in the prank, but I still want to see the look on Deadshot's face.

She's in the candy aisle with a paper bag in her hand, counting out liquorice twists. Her school bag hangs off one shoulder, slipping down her arm. Behind her is a great stack of apple juice that Dopple has been carefully constructing all afternoon. I duck out of sight before she catches a glimpse of me. We don't want her to be alarmed. Instead, I sneak all the way to the other end and loop back around until I'm on the other side of the apple juice. Through a gap in the stack, I can see the back of Deadshot's head, and the two strawberry-blonde braids falling down her back.

She reaches towards a box of chocolate bars when a hand reaches from thin air and grabs hold of her arm. It's Cammie, who's been there the whole time, barely breathing and completely blended in with the rows of candy.

Deadshot shrieks and leaps backwards, right into the stack of apple juice that's been set up to collapse down if anyone bumped into it. The resulting noise is a lot louder than I imagined. It's the sound of so many plastic bottles crashing to the floor, bouncing off each other and ricocheting off the other aisles. The weight of them sends Deadshot to the ground, but it brings more stuff down too, including a whole set of shelves full of cans.

There's even more noise and a rather disturbing creak from above us.

"Poetic justice," is what Dopple told us, but he might have gone overboard with the poetry.

Cammie is half-visible, a look of dawning horror on her face. Dopple pokes his head around the end of the aisle, looking like his entire world has come crashing down around him.

"Get out," he wheezes. "Now."

I'm not sure why he's quite so panicked, but then his mother looms over him. If Dopple looked worried, his mother looks like an angry goddess about to unleash a whole bunch of plagues.

Deadshot comes flailing up out of the mess of bottles and cans. Her face is a furious red and her eyes are wild. She holds a bottle of juice in one hand and is looking right at me.

Oh right. Revenge.

"That's what you get when you mess with us," I shout.

Deadshot flicks her arm back to throw. If there were seconds enough to curse in my head, I definitely would, but there aren't. The plan never accounted for a furious Deadshot. We thought she'd be too humiliated to respond.

Maybe we should have taken a little longer to plan.

I'm going to die from being smacked in the face with a bottle of apple juice. There's no way I can outrun her or—

The end of a rainbow reaches out and tugs me off balance, just as a bottle of apple juice whips past my head. It smashes into the shelf behind me and explodes, showering me in juice and smashing a whole display case of tomato puree.

It looks like a bloodbath, but at least I'm safe, stumbling in the wake of a speeding rainbow girl.

Another bottle whizzes past, smashing through the window in a shower of flying glass. Kel skids around it with me skating helplessly in her wake.

Outside the shop, a handful of passers-by have stopped to stare at the shattered window. It's a mess. Much worse than it's supposed to be. I don't know how Dopple is going to explain this to his mother.

"That was crazy." I'm teetering between panic and hysterical laughter.

"I don't think we're done." Kel grins at me, like this is *exciting* to her.

There's a very small part of me that wants to convince her this is my problem, but it pops inside me like a bubble when Deadshot stands framed in the door.

Kel shoves me away and heads towards the shop. Her feet send bursts of sparks behind her so it looks like she's skating over a rainbow road. She has the biggest grin you've ever seen. "Shottie, for someone whose superpower is accuracy, you miss a *lot*."

Deadshot's response is incoherent, but the anger is clear.

The next bottle she throws at Kel is too fast for me to see. I only see a blur, a rainbow swirl, and then another store window explodes behind us.

"Not good," I say, but Deadshot is racing away from

me. Apparently, I've been forgotten in favour of someone who's backup superpower is being annoying.

Halfway down the street, Kel pauses and bends down as if to tie her shoes.

Deadshot throws one, two, three cans with venomous accuracy. If they hit, I'm pretty sure Kel would be dead because they're almost as fast as bullets. It makes me want to throw up really badly. Luckily, Kel is fast enough that she sprints up the wall and starts dancing her way along the rooftops of the buildings, bouncing in multi-coloured arcs.

"I'll kill you," Deadshot screams, along with some words she probably shouldn't be screaming in public. She runs back into the store, presumably to get more ammunition.

This is way out of control. Whatever plan we had is in ruins, and here I am huddling under one of the tables outside the cafe over the road. Dopple is still in the shop with his furious parents. Cammie's probably invisible from shame or nervousness. If she's not, Deadshot might attack her next. It's not fair for her to get injured on my account. I might not have powers, but I have to do *something*.

I drag myself reluctantly out from under the table and creep towards the shop. I'm trying to avoid the broken glass, but my shoes crunch on it anyway. It's awfully quiet from inside. My heart thumps in my chest. I imagine Deadshot stalking my friends through the store and—

A burst of flame comes pouring out of the open window.

I scream and throw myself on the ground. My face hurts yet again in the same place I banged it yesterday. My hands have skidded among the glass and there's a cut on the base of my hand. A shadow falls over me, blocking out the sun.

I squint up to see a very handsome man with short hair standing over me. One of his hands is glowing and I can feel the heat coming off it.

"Right then," he says. "Are you a witness or a culprit?"

CHAPTER SEVEN

IN WHICH SOMEONE HAS AN IDEA
THAT'S GOING TO CHANGE OUR LIVES

"GLOWSTICK," I gurgle, because here's another superhero. What is with my luck lately? "I'm, uh, well, I'm, uh." It turns out it's very hard to talk to a handsome glowing celebrity who literally helped save the world!

"You're starting to sound very culprit-y." There's a very slight smile curling his lips. "You're Effie, right? Airy's little sib?"

I nod.

"Somehow I don't think you're the one responsible for this but—"

"It wasn't them, Mr. Glowstick." Kel's hands are behind her back, a faint rainbow glow dying away like a halo as she tries to look innocent. "It was all Deadshot's fault."

"Is that right?" A stocky girl around Hazel and Airy's age comes marching out of the shop. Smoke gushes from her nostrils as she twists Deadshot's arm up behind her back. Dragon, another Cute Mutant.

This is bad. We've attracted the attention of people we really shouldn't have.

"Get off me." Deadshot lets out a whole string of terrible names, which I wouldn't call anyone, let alone an actual superhero.

Dragon simply insults Deadshot right back, until I'm blushing fiercely and staring at the ground, wishing it would swallow me up.

"There are children present, Drags," Glowstick says. "Try to be a good influence."

"I stopped this little horror from smacking some poor kid in the face with a can of beans." Dragon gives Deadshot's arm another twist. "That's as good an influence as I get."

"They knocked a pile of stuff down on my head." Deadshot scowls at me. "It was all the baseline's fault. They…" She comes to a sputtering halt when she sees the expression on Glowstick's face.

"I don't like that word." His voice is quiet, but it carries and I would not want to be on the receiving end. "I really, really don't. If I hear you use it again, we'll take you up to the point and you can explain your feelings to Chatterbox and their parent."

"It's just a word. Like a description. A fact. It doesn't mean anything."

"Fine." Glowstick shrugs. His hand looks perfectly normal now. "If it's just a word, call them Effie."

"Okay, whatever." Deadshot sneers. "It's all Effie's fault."

Glowstick and Dragon trade glances for a minute.

"Why don't you all walk me through it then," Glowstick says. "Katie-Kate, you go and round up some people to help with the cleanup."

"Katie-Kate." Dragon gives a very rude gesture, but swaggers away down the street, orange eyes gleaming. Glowstick picks up cafe chairs, and sits us all down in a half-circle. Then the questions start. Eventually, the truth is all spilled, as messy as the ruins of the store.

Glowstick looks like he wants to put his head in his hands. "What a disaster. Deadshot, you and Firewing are clearly the instigating parties in this debacle. However, that initial attack was reported, and being dealt with." He turns his attention to the rest of us. "Ms. Sefo was handling it, so there was no need to turn it into some all-out brawl with epic property damage."

"But we—" Kel says.

"I have two words for you." Glowstick holds up two fingers. "Community. Service."

"That sucks," yelps Kel. "We were just getting Shottie back for literally *attacking someone*."

"We wrecked a lot of stuff." Dopple is very sombre and serious, even for him. "The store needs to be repaired, and food replaced and—"

I can see Kel wants to argue, but she's smart enough to see the look on Glowstick's face and presses her lips together tightly. She settles for scowling at him, which doesn't bother him at all.

In fact, he's smiling. "The twist is that I'm going to make you all do community service together."

I don't know who's more horrified—Deadshot or us.

"You can't!" Kel can't keep quiet anymore. "There's no way! She's a horrible troll of a bigot."

"Then work alongside her and show what tolerance and acceptance are." Glowstick gives us finger guns. It's embarrassing, but I remind myself that he's old. "Together. That's the important part."

Kel moans faintly. "Together. With Shottie."

"Oh, yeah, like you're the one who suffers in this scenario." Deadshot's mouth is fixed in a sneer. "I'm the one stuck hanging out with the stupid misfits club."

"Not the best start, Deadshot." Glowstick shrugs. "You can start by helping clean up around here, but you'll also need something much bigger. Something that gives *back*. I look forward to hearing your proposal. And please, if I hear any more nonsense from any of you—including you, Effie—our next conversation will be less pleasant. I'll let Dragon do the talking, for a start."

"We'll come up with something," Dopple says earnestly. He keeps shooting glances over to the store, as if he fears his mother will come out and encourage Glowstick to give us an even worse punishment.

"I'll be very disappointed if you don't." Glowstick flashes one last smile and saunters away down the street, hands in his pockets.

The instant he's out of sight, Deadshot leaps to her feet. "Wow, I hate you all so much. How is this fair? Being stuck with *you*." She's looking directly at me, but she doesn't say the b-word. Maybe Glowstick got through to her. I wouldn't want to be dragged in front of Chatterbox either.

Kel sneers right back. "You're the one who stalked Effie and attacked them."

Dopple has his head in his hands. "Stop, please. Arguing only makes it worse."

"He's right." Cammie looks around at the street, which is filling up with bystanders. "We need to start cleaning up. And we need ideas about this community service thing."

"The less time I spend with all of you, the better." Deadshot's fingers twitch as if she wants to start hurling things at everyone. "So you better come up with something good."

"Something good?" Kel spins in place, like a rainbow tornado. "I'm going to propose drowning you. That's a service to the community."

"Kel," I say.

"What? I'm not *actually* going to drown her."

"I'd like to see you try." Deadshot crouches down to pick up an *actual sliver of glass* off the street.

My hand reaches out involuntarily and takes hold of her arm. "Both of you stop it."

"Get your hands off me, *Effie*." Deadshot manages to put enough disgust into it that it feels like she's saying baseline, but she drops the glass.

My hand hangs at my side. "Whatever. I'm not happy about spending time with you either, *Shottie*, but here's an idea. We could volunteer to work at Dad's restaurant."

Dopple is still shooting nervous glances at the shop.

"That sounds way too much fun to count. Even if he has us doing dishes, you know he'll let us taste the food. It needs to be something hard, like rebuilding the store."

"They're not going to let a bunch of kids do that," Cammie says. "You need actual skills."

"But we don't have any skills," Dopple moans.

"Speak for yourself," Deadshot snaps back.

Kel stops her spinning, so Deadshot can see the disgusted expression on her face. "The only skills you have are throwing things and annoying people, which will make everything so much worse. Ugh, why did Glowstick have to make us work *together*. Why would he be so cruel?"

"To make us suffer, *obviously*," I say.

"Babysitting," Cammie blurts.

We all turn to look at her, with various expressions of shock and/or horror on our faces.

"It's a good idea," she insists. "Mom is always looking for someone to watch my little sister, and it's usually me, but she's lucky to have two of us. Lots of people here *don't*."

"This may be a good idea," Dopple says. "You know how many people come into the store with little kids. They're all stressed out and you can tell they want a break to get their shopping done in peace."

I frown. "Dad does have to rebook dinner reservations when people can't find anyone to watch their kids."

"No," Deadshot says. "You're all missing the point. If we did this, *we* would have to look after these kids.

There's a kid who lives next door to us who gets all prickly like a hedgehog when he gets mad. Which is, like, *all the time*. We'd have to deal with lil hedgehog boy not wanting to eat his beans just so his parents can go have a fancy dinner at Effie's dumb Dad's dumb restaurant."

"Effie's Dad is not—" Kel begins.

"That's exactly right," Cammie interrupts. "Which is why it's good for community service."

"There are five of us." The idea is starting to make more sense to me. "I think all of us together can deal with one hedgehog kid."

"Four," Deadshot says. "There's no way I'm doing this. Not on my own, not with my friends, and *especially* not with you."

"What do we do?" Dopple asks me helplessly. "If she won't cooperate."

Dragon has returned in the company of a handful of other mutants, most of who look like strong types, although there's one I haven't seen before, with an enormous mouth. Ms. Sefo is there too, but I almost don't recognise her out of the sensible clothes she wears for school. She's in short shorts and a singlet and is transformed into some colossus of muscular steel. It's very disconcerting to see one of your teachers like that. Everybody stares and then tries not to catch each other's eye.

"I'll go talk to Dragon," I say. "Explain the situation, that we've got a great idea and Deadshot doesn't want to help. I'm sure she can do some convincing."

Deadshot gives a rude gesture with each hand,

which is at least better than her throwing things with them. "I hate you all. And I hate this idea." Unspoken is the truth that she'd hate talking to Dragon more.

"So it's a plan?" Cammie grins.

"You actually like this, don't you?" Kel asks. "You want to hang out with annoying little kids."

"They're cute!"

Kel rolls her eyes. "Just don't let Glowstick know you *want* to do this or it might not count as community service."

"I hate it enough for all of us," Deadshot says in a furious voice.

"It's exciting!" Cammie claps her hands together and beams around at us all. "We'll need to advertise! We can put flyers up in the main stores and even leave them at people's houses and—"

Behind her, the mutant with the big mouth gets down on hands and knees. Their lower jaw drops down and they let out an enormous breath, which sends scattered debris flying, piling up in a neat pile along the front wall of the shop.

"Right, kids." Dragon comes up behind Deadshot and claps one hand on her shoulder, making her jump. "Let's get you all working."

CHAPTER EIGHT

OKAY, SO IT TURNS OUT KIDS ARE A LOT OF WORK! WHO KNEW? THIS IS A RHETORICAL QUESTION, DADS

WE SPEND the whole rest of the day cleaning up. The sun has gone down when Glowstick comes back down the street, his hands lit up like twin lamps. Seeing all the work, he looks around with satisfaction. We didn't help much. Between the blowing mutant, one who can melt sand into glass, and Ms. Sefo's strength, we mostly restocked shelves. Oh, and got shouted at by Dopple's mother. She finally ran out of steam and went off to take a bath, and it's been very relaxing since.

The doorbell tinkles as Glowstick enters the shop. He stops just inside the door and turns in a slow circle. "Not bad. I hear you were *all* very helpful. Note my emphasis on all."

Deadshot scowls, because even she knows he's talking about her.

"We have an idea." Cammie is basically bouncing on tiptoes, which is bad, because we're supposed to pretend we hate it. I think the expressions on the rest of our faces make it clear. "We're going to offer to babysit for people. For free."

He smiles at us properly for the first time. "That's… actually a really good idea. I'm impressed. Was that yours?"

Cammie nods, blushes furiously, and begins to fade away.

Glowstick's kind enough to ignore her embarrassment. "I think it's an excellent one. Make a list of all your clients, and I'll check in with them after each time you do it. One tip—don't fight with each other, trash the house, or teach their kids bad language. If it goes well, you might even carry on and make a business out of it."

"We're going to make flyers," Deadshot says, as if it was her idea. "Advertise in stores and hand them out to people's houses."

Glowstick nods. "Look at you, working together. It gives me hope for the future. Let me know when you've got your first client." He gives this funny little salute, and walks out of the store. Deadshot watches him go, and everyone watches Deadshot.

"We're going to make flyers?" Cammie demands. "This was *my* idea."

"Aren't we supposed to be working together?" Deadshot's cheeks flare pink. "I'm pretty okay at design stuff. I can make something that looks good and—"

"Oh my god." Dopple lets out a squawk of laughter. "You've got a crush on Glowstick and you're trying to impress him."

"I am not," Deadshot says furiously.

"I get it." Dopple waggles his eyebrows.

"Shut up or I'll throw something at you."

"Wow, Shottie, what do you do when someone *disagrees* with you?" Kel asks with great interest. "And do you have any other ideas aside from throwing things? You're very boring."

"This is a nightmare," Deadshot says. "I'm going home. I can't deal with you losers anymore."

"Don't dream of Glowstick," Dopple calls, as Deadshot bolts for the door. "He's mine."

Kel snorts and jerks her thumb in the direction of the door. "What are the odds we can work together without me killing her?"

DEADSHOT SURPRISES us the next day by turning up at school with a flyer design that she's carefully inked on a piece of paper.

"You did this?" Kel asks suspiciously when it's slapped down on the table in front of us.

I spin it around so I can read it properly.

Tired? Stressed? Overwhelmed?

Then there are two little cartoons. One's of a man with a kid made of rock hanging off one arm and a shopping bag off the other. The other is of someone with a kid whirling around their head like a tornado. They're fairly simple drawings, but the expressions are so incredibly lifelike that it makes me want to laugh with delight.

Underneath the pictures it says

The Mutantsitters Club
Available now.
No job too big or small.
We work for free!
Reliable. Trustworthy. Experienced.

Then there are little cartoon versions of our faces, which in some miracle, Deadshot hasn't made look ridiculous. She's actually nailed all of us, from Kel's grin and rainbow halo to the anxious wrinkle between Dopple's eyebrows.

"It's amazing," I say, looking up at her. "Seriously."

"I know it's amazing." The sneer is back. "I didn't come here for validation."

"Shottie, I've finally figured out your real mutant power," Kel says. "You miss too much for it to be accuracy, so it's obviously a complete inability to take a compliment."

"Yeah, well your mutant ability is being an annoying brat, and yet somehow you're still better than Effie, who doesn't have one at all."

My mouth twitches. How can she make me feel this small? What did I ever do to her? I want to screw the flyer up or tear it into tiny pieces, but instead I lock my feelings down and slide it back over the desk.

"Whatever," I say. "Run off some copies of your little pictures and Kel can whiz around and deliver them."

"My amazing pictures," Deadshot says.

"Sure. Just like you're reliable, trustworthy and experienced."

She snatches the flyer back and stalks away.

"I hate her," Kel says. "I really, actually do. I'm going to throw her off the waterfall or—"

"Forget it." I slump in my seat. "The flyer is good. It'll get clients. We can do some babysitting, do our community service, and then we never have to see Deadshot again."

"If I accidentally kill her, don't blame me," Kel says darkly.

THE FLYERS DO WORK, almost like a miracle. It's that afternoon when we get our first inquiry. Funnily enough, it's the hedgehog kid that lives next door to Deadshot.

"Oh!" The woman who answers the door is tall and dark skinned, wearing a headscarf. "You're all here."

"This is a team effort, ma'am," Cammie says.

"Spike will be delighted. The more playmates the better. Please come in. I'm Dahlia, one of the fertility mutants."

She's not joking. This is one of the neighbourhoods where the houses are built instead of grown, but you wouldn't know from the interior. Every surface is covered in plants, vines winding up the roof and blooms sprouting everywhere.

"Apologies, it's an occupational hazard, but at least it smells nice." She leads us through into the kitchen and shows us where the food is stored. All the cupboards and drawers are labelled with words grown in tiny flowers. "Don't worry too much if he doesn't eat all his dinner. He's fussy at the best of times. Here's the number where you can contact me, as well as the doctor. Now, where is that kid?"

We eventually find him in the upstairs loft room, which is strewn with toys amongst the grass and flowers that carpet the entire space. He's curled up in a ball under the bed, and we can see nothing but prickles.

"The sitters are here." Dahlia gets down on hands and knees. "Don't you want to meet them?"

There's a mumble from under the bed.

"He does get shy." She gets back to her feet awkwardly. "He'll warm up, or at least come out for a snack. Are you okay for me to leave, or wait until he appears?"

"It'll be fine," Cammie says with a big smile. "My little sister is the same. I'm used to it."

"Honestly, that's such a relief." Dahlia laughs. "Glowstick said you'd do an excellent job, and it's been a long time since I had the break. I really appreciate it."

We all mutter about how it's fine and no problem. It doesn't sound like good advertising to explain why we're doing it, but given the way gossip works on the island, she probably already knows. It's nice Glowstick put himself out for us, but it also makes me feel guilty, like we have to do a really good job.

Dahlia finally lets herself out the front door and

walks down the path to meet another pair of mutants. One of them is Feral, who catches my eye and gives me an enormous, toothy smile. Part of me wants to run after her and ask what happened in the forest, but it's in front of people and besides, we have work to do.

I head back upstairs to find Cammie and Kel trying to coax the kid out from under the bed. Cammie is picking at a cupcake while Kel dangles her hand over the edge of the bed, swishing it back and forth so it streams rainbows.

Spike has uncurled slightly, the quills around his head retracting. His eyes flit from Kel to the cupcake and back again.

I slide down the wall to sit beside Cammie. "I'll have that if you don't want it."

She holds the plate out towards me, and almost immediately a head comes sliding out from under the bed.

"Can I share?"

"Come downstairs, and you can have your very own," Cammie says, wide-eyed, as if this is the best offer anyone could get.

The rest of the kid comes wriggling out. As he gets to his feet, the spines all down his back retract, leaving a Pikachu onesie that's perforated with a whole lot of tiny holes. "How many cupcakes are there?" He's very serious, as if he's about to perform a bunch of complicated cupcake calculus.

"Enough for everyone." Cammie pops a chunk into her mouth. "I'm Cammie. What's your name?"

"Spike. You know that because you talked to my Mom."

"Yes." Cammie smiles. "But it's polite to introduce yourself. Like this is Effie, and this rainbow girl here is called Kel."

"Pretty," Spike says.

"I prefer devastatingly beautiful." Kel waves one rainbow hand.

The kid looks her up and down with a slight frown. "You're weird."

I give a yelp of laughter, and Kel punches me hard on the shoulder. I'm rubbing it and Spike is laughing as we leave the bedroom.

"Boo!" Deadshot drops from the ceiling.

I scream. Cammie drops her cupcake. Kel lashes out with fists and swear words.

And Spike curls into a small and spiky ball.

"What are you *doing*?" Kel blurs through the air, appearing behind Deadshot and shoving her hard.

Deadshot stumbles, bounces off the wall, and falls face down onto the kid we're supposed to be babysitting. She lets out a terrifying shriek and flings herself off him. Her face and forearms have quills jutting out.

"Um, excuse me, but what is going on?" Dopple calls from downstairs.

"This is the worst start to our baby-sitting career." Cammie wrings her hands miserably.

Deadshot is pressed up against the wall, waving her arms around like she's on fire.

I crouch beside her. I'm nervous, but someone has to help her. "Stop flailing and let me get them out."

"Get out of my face." There are tears rolling down her cheeks.

"Can you please dial the dramatics down for five seconds?" I steal this line from Dad Adé, who used to use it a lot on Airy.

Deadshot says nothing, so I reach out gently and tug one quill free. She whimpers.

Kel peers over my shoulder. "She deserves them, scaring the poor kid like that."

Deadshot winces. "You don't know anything, Kaleidoscope. That's a game I've heard him play. Him and his Mom sneak up on each other like tigers in the jungle or something. Ouch, Effie, be *gentle*."

"He *chooses* to play that," Cammie says. "He doesn't have some mad stranger jumping out at him when he's excited about a cupcake."

"I was *trying* to be nice." There are tears in Deadshot's eyes. "Do I ever get any credit for—Ouch, Effie, can you *please* be careful? It's like you're deliberately trying to make it hurt."

"I could take over." Kel grins.

Deadshot groans. "I hate you. All of you, but especially you, Kel."

"Whatever will I do about my broken heart?" Kel reaches down and tweaks one of the quills. Deadshot lets out an inarticulate yelp and shoves off from the wall, ignoring the ones still in her face to chase Kel down the stairs. There's another series of thumps and a very loud Dopple-like yelp.

"Why does this always happen to me?" Dopple

cries. "I think I broke my arm. Deadshot, why are you the worst?"

Cammie puts her face in her hands. "This is never going to work."

Spike uncurls himself slightly to reveal two wide and staring eyes. "I'm telling my Mom on you."

CHAPTER NINE

WHOSE IDEA WAS THIS WHOLE MUTANTSITTING CLUB ANYWAY?

BY THE TIME Dahlia actually gets home, Spike is asleep, his silence bought with cupcakes and lemonade. Kel and Deadshot are on opposite sides of the lounge, sitting on their phones and ignoring everyone else. It's the only way we have any kind of peace as Dopple, Cammie and I play a board game.

"Wow, this is so peaceful." Dahlia takes off her shoes and places them carefully beside the door. "I was a little worried I'd come back to chaos. You even tidied everything up. What service."

Deadshot raises an eyebrow but keeps her face down. The welts are mostly gone because Dopple did some research and found some plants which soothe skin conditions. Hopefully Dahlia doesn't notice we took any. Given the literally thousands of plants in this house, surely she can't keep track of all them, mutant powers or not.

"He's a sweetheart," Cammie says.

"I checked on him ten minutes ago, and he's sleeping peacefully," Dopple adds.

"Aren't you all delightful?" Dahila's gaze travels across all of us, even Deadshot. "We'll definitely have to do this again. And I'll make sure to tell all my friends with children. Let's get this community service project going nicely."

Cammie and I exchange worried glances. If this goes too smoothly, it might not count.

"No, it's fine. Glowstick and I are close, and he let me know you might need a little head start. But given that you managed to charm my little Spiky, I think you'll be just fine." She gives us a wink, and I wonder how much she managed to figure out.

We finish up the board game, and then Dahlia sends us on our way with cupcakes, which she assures us don't count as payment. We pause at the end of the path, looking back at the house.

"That wasn't terrible," Cammie says. "Not by the end."

"Speak for yourself." Deadshot prods at her face, but she doesn't even wince. "Maybe Kel can stay home next time."

"You're the nightmare who scares children," Kel smirks. "All I did was teach you a lesson."

Cammie and Dopple take the opportunity to leave, but I stay with Kel because we live near each other and I don't want to walk home alone or, even worse, with Deadshot.

"I've had enough of your lessons, Kaleidoscope." Deadshot flings one of the little wooden people from the game at Kel. She must have pocketed it. Kel darts out of the way.

"You'll always be far too slow for me, Shottie. Find a new game, I'm bored of this one."

"I hate you all," Deadshot says. "I'm going home."

She strides off down the street, the moonlight making her hair glow.

Kel shakes her head. "She really is the most annoying person in existence."

"I know." I shove my hands in my pockets, and turn to walk home, but Kel is still staring after Deadshot. She carries on watching until the other girl rounds the corner and disappears.

"Oh my god," I say. "You like her."

"What? No? What? Don't be ridiculous." She punches me in the arm again.

"Kel, that's a *terrible* idea. You can't like *Deadshot*!"

"Good, because it's quite the opposite."

"I hope so." I stare at her face, trying to see if she's blushing.

"So little faith in me, Eff. If I ever like Deadshot, you have permission to hit me on the head with a rock until I regain my sanity."

"I might hold you to that."

"You won't have to." She shoves me, so hard I almost fall over, but she's oddly quiet on the way home, as if she's thinking about Deadshot instead of joking like normal.

DAHLIA WASN'T LYING about spreading the word. We get so many inquiries that we end up booked for three weeks in advance. Glowstick swings by my house while we're having a planning meeting.

"Look at you all hard at work," he says. "And nobody's hit anyone or smashed a window."

The tips of Dopple's ears go pink. I'm not entirely sure I get the Glowstick thing. I understand how he's very good-looking, obviously, but he's also kind of old.

"Kel did slam my face into a prickly baby," Deadshot drawls.

"She tripped." Kel matches the tone exactly.

"And yet we have a satisfied customer," Glowstick says. "The kid asked to see you again. He said, and I quote, *even the scary one.*"

"Oh Shottie," Kel says. "You have your very first fan. How does it feel?"

I almost snap at her to stop flirting, but Glowstick is watching us all with this tiny smile, as if he finds the show secretly hilarious.

He reaches out and twists Cammie's proposed schedule around. "This might actually keep you out of trouble. Keep up this pace, and we can call this done by the end of the month."

"Great," Deadshot says. "Then I don't have to spend another second with these people."

"You never know. They might grow on you." Glowstick heads for the door.

"Where's the schedule?" Dopple asks. "Who's up first?"

"The Lopez family," Cammie says. "They've got two kids, but only one of them's powered."

"A friend for Effie," Deadshot says, half under her breath.

"The mutant kid's power is to generate an electrical field while they sleep. It means you can charge your phone off them. This one should be easy."

And it is. The human kid is eight years old. He's needy and constantly wants stories and games, but that's something I can actually do. I like reading out loud, and doing the different voices for the different characters, and the others end up listening too. I even catch Deadshot actually glancing in my direction.

Unfortunately, that's the easiest babysitting gig we get for a while. It turns out looking after kids with powers is harder than you'd think.

THE NEXT KID turns into stone. It takes three of us to carry her upstairs to bed and when we drop her on Cammie's foot, Kel has to go whizzing off to fetch Doc to get her shattered toes healed up. The kid is upset by all the fuss and changes back to flesh which is much easier for a while. Until she climbs up on a glass coffee table and turns back to stone. It makes for an incredible noise and sends glass and wood flying everywhere. We have to roll the kid off to bed, except Dopple rolls her too far, and she goes thumping down the stairs, smashing half of them.

Luckily, when the parents turn up they're not even mad.

"I told you we should have replaced the coffee table," one of them said. "I saw her up there the other day, and I knew it would be trouble."

"And I *asked* you to call the guy about reinforcing the stairs."

"I did! They didn't have any free slots for two weeks."

"Things were so much easier when she couldn't climb."

They look so sad that we don't even tell them about Cammie's toes, and make our escape as quickly as we can.

"Some people are the worst," Deadshot says. "Why put your kid made of rock in a bedroom upstairs? And you shouldn't have *anything* made of glass."

"Are your toes okay?" I ask Cammie.

She waggles them in her sandals. "Good as new."

"Can't get much worse than tonight, can it?" Kel claps me on the shoulder.

Everyone screeches at her for being a jinx. Even Deadshot joins in.

EVERYTHING SEEMS great with the next kid, a four year old girl called Sol. It's a daytime sitting job, so we get to take her on an outing. The kid is super friendly and even though she runs everywhere, we've got a super-speedy person to catch her. We take her to the beach, and let her chase us around the sand for a while. Then she demands to go in the water.

"We didn't bring your bathing suit, sweetie," Cammie says.

She pulls her trouser legs up. "I can paddle."

"There are five of us," Kel says. "We can manage one kid."

"What's her power, anyway?" I ask.

"They didn't fill out the form properly," Dopple says. "I assume she lights up or glows or shines at night, because her name's Sol, like the sun god."

"If she starts boiling the water, I'll drag her out." Kel leads her down towards the water.

The kid tugs her hand free and runs towards the waves. Kel scoots ahead of her and splashes into the ocean to stop Sol going too deep. The rest of us follow behind.

Except the instant the kid enters the water, she trips and falls face down.

Kel darts for her and we splash after.

"I've got her." Kel grabs for the kid's shirt and hauls it up out of the water. All she's holding is a soaked piece of clothing. I make a grab for the pants, but they're also empty. Dopple throws himself bodily into the waves after her cap, as if somehow she'll be in there.

"What's going on?" Cammie squeals.

"Where did she go?" Deadshot turns in a circle. "She was right there."

"She vanished." I'm on my knees in the water,

flailing my arms around. "She's invisible. Try to find an invisible kid." A wave hits me in the chest and sends me backwards. I taste salt in my mouth and spit.

"Quiet!" Dopple shouts. "Listen for her."

"If she's invisible, why are her clothes empty?" Deadshot asks.

I have to admit, that's a decent question.

"So what?" Kel asks. "She just disappeared?"

"We've lost a kid," Cammie groans. "This is very, very bad."

"This can't be happening." I tug on my hair. "Something else is going on. They would have *warned* us about this. Dopple, where's the sheet of paper with the details?"

He fishes in his pocket, but what he pulls out is a sodden, unreadable mess. "Sol for soluble." There's a hysterical edge to his voice. "She dissolves in water."

"Even more reason for them to warn us." I think I'm crying, and I'm not the only one. "Dopple, how do we un-dissolve her?"

"I don't know! It's not a thing you usually do. Maybe if we evaporate the water?"

"What?" Kel screams. "Evaporate the entire ocean?"

"We need Glowstick," Dopple says. "He can generate enough heat."

"There's no way we're telling him," Deadshot says. "I'm not starting this over again."

"It'll be a lot worse if they found out we dissolved a kid," I scream at her.

"They should have left instructions." Deadshot crosses her arms over her chest.

"I'm sure they'll see it—" I begin.

"Whee!" A delighted child's voice sounds from above us.

We all tilt our heads towards the sky. A small child is falling towards us.

"Catch," Dopple screeches. Both Kel and Deadshot rush forward. Kel bounces off Deadshot's shoulder and goes sprawling into the water. I almost close my eyes, because I can't watch this, but Deadshot plucks the child casually out of the air.

"Don't dip her into the water," Dopple shouts.

"I do have *some* brains." Deadshot holds the child high and strides confidently back to shore.

"She must have evaporated and condensed in the air or something," Dopple says.

I elbow him in the side. "Oh, sure. Pretend you know how it works."

We get her dressed on the beach and head for home. At least the kid seems perfectly happy.

"What do they do when it rains?" Dopple asks, full of curiosity now that the panic is gone. "And how do they bathe her? Just let her reconstitute in the ceiling after every shower?"

"Shut your mouth and forget your questions," Deadshot snaps. "We're not asking or saying a thing, just in case. There's no way this is coming back on us."

But once again, the parents are so grateful for a break, they don't ask any questions. Guess my life is luckier than I thought. Hopefully I'm not jinxing it.

CHAPTER TEN

IN WHICH WE MEET THE MOST FAMOUS CHILDREN ON THE ISLAND AND SOMEHOW AVOID DISASTER

AFTER THE DISSOLVING CHILD INCIDENT, we're a lot more careful about asking questions about the powers of the children we babysit. We also do a lot less unplanned activities. Everything has to be run past the parents. It's possible we're getting good at this.

Glowstick is very pleased with our progress. He's also asked us to keep this evening free, which makes us very nervous. We're supposed to meet at my house at seven, but we've all been assembled here since six, eating leftovers and unable to sit still.

"Maybe he's going to free us from our burden." Deadshot is lounging in my favourite chair with her legs up over the side. "It's about time, too. I'm sick of all your faces."

"I don't think so," Dopple says. "Why would he come to Effie's house for that? We'd meet him somewhere in town."

"Maybe he wants to pat you on the head and say

you've been a very good boy," Deadshot sneers. "Make you pass out from unrequited love."

"I don't love him," Dopple snaps. "I just think he looks good."

There's a loud knock at the door and we all freeze.

"You open it," I tell Kel.

"It's not my house." She hugs her knees and eyes the door warily.

"It's not going to be a monster," Deadshot sighs. "Honestly, you're such annoying brats."

"Then why aren't you answering it?" Kel asks.

"Because it's not my weird treehouse." Deadshot makes the rude gesture she's so fond of.

"Fine." I sigh theatrically, in the hope that someone will intervene. "I'll do it."

Nobody else offers to save me, and we all sit there awkwardly until the knock sounds again. I finally leap up out of the couch and jog awkwardly over to the door.

When I swing it open, my eyes almost burst out of my head.

There's a person on the front doorstep with greenish skin and big eyes. There's a lotus flower at the hollow of their throat, and more blooms form delicate lines on their skin like intricate tattoos.

It's Chatterbox. Standing on my doorstep. The famous and terrifying one. Although right now they're scruffy-looking in a hoodie and ripped jeans, with battered rainbow sneakers.

There's a little anxiety crease in their forehead, just

like Dopple's, and it makes them about fifty percent less scary. "Hi. You're Effie, right?"

"Um." It's hard to breathe. "I mean, yes. I am."

They give a half-smile and turn around. "It *is* the right house, Dani. I think this counts as you being wrong."

"Honestly." Probably the most beautiful person I've ever seen comes walking up the path. Her skin is darker than Chatterbox's, but she's draped in even more flowers. Petals scatter behind her, caught by the wind that whips the soft vines of her hair. Marvellous. The other half of Biome, and also somehow walking towards my house.

What really surprises me is the child hanging off each arm.

"You're the mutantsitters, right?" Chatterbox asks. "I mean these brats aren't mutants, but—"

"Mum says it's rude to call us brats," one child says.

Chatterbox snorts. "Does she? That's very considerate of her. There are other words I sometimes want to use, but I'm running out of vocabulary."

"Do you mean—?" The other child asks.

"Don't say it," Marvellous says.

The children drop down from her arms, and run over to Chatterbox. They both hide behind their parent and peer out at me. Marvellous joins them and they make a strange and beautiful family portrait together.

"Hi, I'm Dani," Marvellous says. "And this is Dylan. These are our two children, who'll hopefully remember their manners and—"

"I'm Willow." The two children look very similar,

but one who speaks first has more blue and purple flowers in their short hair, and skin that's a slightly paler green.

"And I'm Soo-yeon." The other has a halo of luminous pink lotus flowers and blinks hazel eyes at me, still mostly hiding.

"Um, okay. Cool. Hi." Help, this is terrible. I need to find some words, preferably polite ones. "My name's Effie." I swing the door to the house wider, hoping to find some distractions, but all my friends have made themselves scarce.

Probably assuming we're in trouble.

"Sorry." I swallow hard. "I'm, um, shy. It's nice to meet you, Biome, and your children too."

"We're not *really* their children." Willow blinks at me and then peers up at Chatterbox. "We're spooky monsters, but we're made from their DNA so we're still family anyway, aren't we?"

"Yes." Chatterbox plants a kiss on their child's petal-strewn head. "Family's what you make it, after all."

"We've got a lot of aunties," Soo-yeon explains solemnly. "And one uncle."

"Big, big family." Chatterbox winks. "Now do you two spooky monsters want to meet the rest of your new sitters?"

The rest of my so-called friends are poking their heads around the corner, totally not sneaky at all. They try to hide when Chatterbox notices them, but the two kids go running into the house. Seconds later, they're trying to guess who is who and demanding to see demonstrations of everyone's power. I wonder what their attitude is to baselines.

"Don't be fooled," Dani says. "They look sweet, but they're adept at twisting people around their little vine-fingers. Believe about a third of what they tell you, and never listen to any plans they come up with."

"How do I know which third?" I ask.

"When we figure that out, we'll tell you." Dylan grins at me. "They're a f... a friendly handful, that's for sure. You'll probably be fine, because I think meeting five new people is enough of a novelty to distract them. If you get stuck, do feats of strength or something."

I blink at them. "Feats of strength?"

"Yeah, like a powers competition. Have your rainbow friend give them a running race. That'll keep them occupied and tire them out at the same time."

Great, and what can I do? Run in a circle like a slow and useless human and let them laugh at what people looked like before evolution took over?

"It'll be fine." Dani's looking at the two of them fondly as they chatter at full speed to the others. "They're sweet kids, really, just..."

"Intense," Dylan suggests. "Usually we have one of the gang look after them, but we're getting the whole group together for the first time since the kids arrived."

"If they're really difficult, threaten them with Aunt Violet," Dani says. "She's the only one they're actually intimidated by. Even Katie's too much of a soft touch. And if anything goes wrong, the kids know how to contact us through the grapevine."

"Oh," I say.

"It's a plant thing." Dylan shrugs. "But it'll be fine. I feel like we're scaring you off."

Dani nudges Dylan. "They're actually rather delightful."

"Most of the time." Dylan claps their hands together. "Willow! Soo-yeon! Come give us a hug."

The two children scamper over and throw their arms around their parents, who both crouch down to look into their eyes.

"Remember what we talked about?" Dani asks.

"Best behaviour," they say in unison, but they giggle at the end.

Dylan plants a kiss on each child's cheek. "Yes, or else…"

"Dark and unspecified consequences!" They say it with far too much excitement.

"How old are they?" I ask.

Dani pulls a face. "Like, a month? They were born chattering like this, which has been a learning curve." She transfers her attention back to the children. "We have to leave now, okay? We won't be too long."

"Just drinking and catching up with the gang," Willow says with a sigh. "Reminiscing about life as a cute mutant."

It sounds so unlike a kid that it startles a giggle out of me.

Dylan favours me with a jaded look. "They're always like this. You'll see. Remember, call if you need anything at all."

"We'll be fine! They don't, like, dissolve in water or anything, do they?"

"No, they do swipe things with their vine arms, but we'll check them before they leave so they don't steal the valuables."

"Vine arms?" I glance at the twins, but their arms look normal to me.

"They shoot them out like Spider-Man. Thwip thwip, except vines." Dylan shoots a little one at me from their own hand. It brushes the hair off my face and then disappears back into their sleeve.

"We'll be *fine*," Soo-yeon says.

Willow rolls their eyes. "Yeah, stop worrying. It's nice to spend time with people closer to our age instead of a million boring adults."

Soo-yeon grins at their sibling. "Say that around Auntie Feral, I dare you."

"I will!"

"Whatever. You're not brave enough."

"Good luck." Dylan says to me, and heads down the path with Dani. At the end, they turn and look back, but Dani tugs them away.

"Wow," Dopple says from behind me. "Hogging Biome all to yourself."

I turn in the doorway. "You could have come and introduced yourself."

"To *them?*"

"They're just people," Deadshot says.

"Wrong," Willow says. "They're aliens like us. But not scary ones."

"Unless you're a villain," Soo-yeon puts in. "Then they're very, very scary."

"Those are just *stories*. I bet Auntie Feral is exaggerating about half of it."

"Auntie Fetch doesn't exaggerate, and she says the same things."

"Either way." Willow eyeballs Deadshot. "Don't be mean to us. That's the rule."

"We won't," Cammie says. "We're here to look after you and have fun. So, what would you like to do first?"

Their first suggestion is to jump off the waterfall, but we manage to detour them into playing a board game. The problem is that they cheat, and they're really good at it. They've got some sleight of hand going on with their vine-fingers and none of us are quite sure what they're doing.

"It's statistically incredibly unlikely you'd roll thirteen sixes in a row," Dopple says in exasperation.

"Do we have luck powers, Will?"

"It sounds more like Dopple has sore loser powers." Willow tosses the dice in the air and we watch as they all come down as sixes. "Or is really bad at throwing dice."

"It's not a thing you can be good or bad at." Dopple's face is turning red.

"It seems like we're a lot better at it then you," Sooyeon says.

"Let's do something else." I push my chair back from the table. "A different kind of competition. We'll set up a target and see who can throw most accurately."

Deadshot looks at me like I've grown a second head. "Uh, Effie?"

"Just trust me," I snap.

"Fine. Let me go home and get my practice target. Then we can all play." She smirks around the room, and then saunters out.

"One of us needs to beat her," Kel says. "That's the only way to shut her up. So cheating is on the table. I wonder if I can run to the target and back without her noticing? Or Cammie can go invisible and sneak up to put it in there?"

"Nobody's cheating," I say with a meaningful look at the two kids, who are both sitting there with innocent expressions on their faces. "This is going to be like a powers competition, that's all."

"Yes." Soo-yeon grins. "We want to give rainbow dash here a race, too."

"You want to race me?" Kel frowns.

"We could do it while we wait for the angry one to get back." Both kids have expressions on their faces that make me suspicious.

"You realise I have *super-speed*," Kel says.

"We know we can't beat you." Willow rolls their eyes again.

"It's about seeing how close we can get."

"Fine, why not." Kel gets to her feet. "We can do a race down the path, to the end of the road and back again. First person to touch the front door wins."

Cammie touches my arm, as we follow her out of the house. "This seems like a terrible idea."

"It was Chatterbox's suggestion," I tell her, and she falls silent.

Soon, everyone is standing in the front garden aside from the plant kids flanking Kel on the front porch. All three of them have cocky smirks on their faces.

"On your marks." I take a deep breath. "Get set... go."

Kel flashes off in a blur. Willow and Soo-yeon extend their arms like whips and catch hold of the fence posts. They use these to slingshot themselves forward, and two green blurs fly off after Kel. They're briefly visible on the street, before they send themselves hurtling forward again.

"Hope nobody gets hurt." Cammie hugs herself, already beginning to fade into the greenery.

I don't even get time to answer, because a rainbow blur appears at the end of the driveway. Kel becomes visible as she decelerates to turn the corner. I'm expecting to see her turn back into a blur again, but she comes to a dead stop.

There's a green rope wrapped around her middle, stopping her from moving.

"What the—?" She grabs at it, but Soo-yeon jogs past her, panting theatrically.

"Ding." The first twin slaps their hand on the door. "Looks like I win."

Willow slingshots into view, almost crashing into Kel. They disentangle their vine arm from around Kel and look up with a grin. "Sorry."

"You cheated," Kel splutters. "You can't grab someone!"

"Nobody said there were *rules*," Soo-yeon leans against the door.

"It's not in the spirit of racing!"

"What's that?" Willow asks with great interest.

Kel jabs her finger in our direction. "Nobody tell Deadshot about this."

"Oh, don't worry." I grin. "I wouldn't want to spoil the surprise. It's her turn next."

CHAPTER ELEVEN

REMEMBER THE LAST CHAPTER? LIKE THAT, BUT EVERYTHING GOES MUCH, MUCH WORSE

DEADSHOT FINALLY RETURNS with the target, which is enormous and has a whole bunch of circles on it, each with a point value. The bullseye in the middle is almost too small to see.

"Every time." She taps it with a smirk.

Kel snorts "Set it up against the house and prove it."

When we all stand back in a row, I can't even see the center. There's no way I'm going to make it. I'm hoping I can hit the target at all. Deadshot gives everyone three darts.

"I'll give a demonstration first," she says lazily.

She snaps off all three darts one after the other. They arrow through the air. I don't even watch her. I pay attention to the kids instead. Willow has a smirk on their face as Soo-yeon's hand flickers. Three tendrils of green vine go shooting out, faster than Deadshot's darts. They make the barest green flicker in the air as they move on an interception course.

One dart lands about halfway towards the center, one hits the very edge and the last slams into the side of the house.

"Wow," Kel says. "Deadly accurate."

Deadshot whirls around and glares at us. "What was that? Something interfered."

"I didn't see anything." I blink at her. "You just didn't get the target."

"I. Don't. Miss."

"It's fine." Kel tosses her own dart in the air. "We'll let you try again. Everyone can have a practice throw."

Deadshot stalks over and removes her darts. "If any of you try to use your powers... was it you, Chameleon?"

Cammie shrugs. "I was standing right here."

Deadshot throws again. This time, not a single dart hits the target. "Who was it?" She rounds on the rest of us. "Was it you two little brats? Did you touch my darts?"

"Of course it was us." Willow raises an eyebrow. "We're finding the flaw in your powers. The slightest bit of interference and you miss."

Deadshot's fist clenches at her side. She snatches a dart out of Dopple's hand and hurls it at the target. Willow snatches it from the air with a vine and whips it right back towards Deadshot. It hovers in front of her face.

"I mean, they're *fine* powers," Soo-yeon says. "They're good for some things, but they've got limitations. All powers do."

"At least I have powers," Deadshot sneers. "Unlike Effie here, who's a stupid baseline."

The twins' expressions change instantly. They're not sweet flower children anymore. I'm reminded of the old trees in the forest, and Cybele rustling out from between them. They've even grown taller.

"That's an interesting choice of words," Willow says.

"They *are*." Despite the warning signs, Deadshot doesn't back down. "Effie's human. No powers at all. Evolution skipped them because—"

Willow flicks out both arms in the direction of Deadshot, wrapping vines tightly around her. She flails and tries to call for help, but it comes out as a strangled gasp.

The rest of us have no idea what to do. This doesn't seem *good*, but at the same time, it's not like Deadshot didn't deserve it.

Willow hoists Deadshot into the air. "Do you want to play catch, Soo-yeon?"

Their sibling smiles. "I'd love to." They dash across to the other side of the front yard.

We're all standing there watching helplessly as Deadshot spins through the air and into the waiting vines of Soo-yeon.

"The thing is," Willow says. "Our Grandpear is a so-called baseline, and so is our Halmeoni. We love them and would do anything for them. Implying that people without powers are lesser is… I'm struggling for words, Soo-yeon. Do you have any?"

Soo-yeon hurls Deadshot back in Willow's direction. "Only ones that Mum would hate us using. Pear would know what to say. They're very good at that."

Willow snatches Deadshot out of the air and dangles her upside down. "Technically, we don't have powers. This is how we're built. I don't think that's what you mean though, is it? You're saying Effie isn't as good because they're not a *mutant*. There's no reason that humans and mutants and plants like us can't get along."

"Aside from one reason." Soo-yeon reaches out and grabs hold of Deadshot as if they're playing tug-of-war with her. "Hatred. It's a virus and one that nearly killed your people. Why would you do your part to keep it going?"

"Who *are* these kids?" Dopple mutters.

Kel basically has little stars in her eyes. "I don't care, but I've never seen anything so beautiful in my life."

Willow and Soo-yeon release Deadshot, who staggers, falls to her knees, and promptly throws up.

"Oops." Soo-yeon grimaces. "We might have gone overboard, Will."

I run into the house for cold water and a damp cloth, then crouch down beside Deadshot. "Are you okay?"

She shakes her head.

"Here." I place the cloth on her forehead and tip the glass to her mouth. She drinks shakily, although a bunch spills down her front.

Willow waves their vines in our direction. "See? This is evolution. Much more than your throwing powers. Effie, who you've been rude to, is the one looking after you."

Kel joins on Deadshot's other side. "Come on. Let's get you inside where you can lie down."

THE REST of the sitting job is remarkably quiet. The plant kids are docile and barely even cheat when we play games again. By the time Dylan and Dani turn back up, the twins are curled on the couch together, reading quietly.

"Is this magic?" Dani asks. "What did you do to our children?"

Dylan smirks. "It's guilt, isn't it? I recognise it on their little faces. It looks like innocence, but it's not."

Dani puts her hand on her hips. "Did you two do something? Tell the truth please, or we'll have to bring Auntie Fetch in."

"They were delightful," Kel says.

"Everything was fine, really. No problem at all." I really don't want to lose our highest profile clients, and Deadshot did have it coming.

"We threw the mean girl around," Willow says. "After she said the b-word."

"We made her feel sick like she made us feel sick," Soo-yeon adds. "She deserved it and we could have done a *lot* more, but we didn't. And then we were very good after that."

"We also won a running race against Rainbow

Dash." Willow beams at their parents with that dazzling smile.

"Cheaters," Kel says through a cough.

"You okay, Deadshot?" Dylan doesn't sound entirely interested in the answer.

"Fine." She doesn't even look up from her phone.

"Perhaps don't use words like that around our kids. Or us." The smile Dylan offers sends chills down my spine. "For your sake more than anything." They catch Dani's eye. "Not that I'm condoning violence in response."

The kids leap up and throw their arms around their parents. "We're very sorry and next time we'll try something else! Like dangling her very gently over the waterfall."

"You can't say things like that about our Grandpear, and Halmeoni, Mum. That's the problem. It's bigotry, and you said that needs to be challenged."

"We'll talk about this later," Dani says, "but using violence sometimes makes things worse."

Willow scowls. "But we don't *have* mind control. It would be much more efficient if we did. Just a little spore to burrow into her brain and fix things."

"That's even worse, you menaces," Dylan says. "No spores or mind control allowed. Ever."

The twins subside onto the couch, tangling their vines together and muttering.

Dylan turns their attention to me. "So the Mutantsitters Club survived this—mostly, at least. Is there any chance you'd do it again?"

"Please?" Dani asks. "We'll put in a very good word with Glowstick."

"I'm in," Kel says. "For sure. We need a rematch."

Dopple and Cammie agree as well.

"Whatever," Deadshot says. "This'll get it done faster, which is all I want. For this miserable experience to be over and done with, and to never see these people again."

"See, Mum," Willow says in a loud whisper. "She's rude, even though Effie and Kel looked after her when she was sick. She always acts like she's better than them."

Deadshot says nothing except we can all see how pink her cheeks and ears are.

"We should take these two home to bed." Dylan holds up both hands before the twins can start up any racket. "No, I won't hear any complaints. You'll get to come here again, and next time there won't be any throwing of people."

ON OUR SECOND sitting appointment for the plant kids, they're weirdly subdued. They don't even try to cheat when we're playing games, and express no interest in a rematch against Kel. She's very disappointed.

"Do you think someone broke them?" She peers through into the living room, where they're sitting on the couch and talking quietly.

"I'm guessing they got told to behave."

"We're tired," Willow pronounces, from their spot on the couch. The siblings are tangled together so it's hard to tell them apart.

"Is there somewhere we can sleep?" Soo-yeon blinks huge hazel eyes at us. "We could try here on the couch, but—"

"No," I say. "You can use my room of course."

"But it's *your* room," Willow says.

"Better than Airy's," I tell them.

"You don't mind petals all through your bed?"

I shake my head with a smile. "It'll smell nice. Come on." I cross to the couch and hold my hands out. "Let me show you."

With the way they talk and act, it's easy to forget how small they are. They seem very docile and childlike as they put their hands in mine. I lead them down the hallway to my room.

Willow beams at me. "Oh, look! You have a moss bed."

"Yeah, it's the original one that was grown here. It's very soft."

"We know. It's the only way we sleep properly." Soo-yeon goes bouncing into the bed and Willow follows. They curl up like a yin/yang symbol, entwining their vine-hands around each other. It's sweet.

"I don't trust them," Deadshot says from behind me. "They're planning a prank."

"Doesn't seem likely." I stand in the doorframe and watch them nestle in together.

"They hate me." Her voice is low. "They want to make me suffer."

I glance over my shoulder, to see Deadshot fiddling with her hair. "They're a couple of kids."

"Vindictive, malicious kids. They're monsters, not even human *or* mutant."

"Wow, Shottie." I pull the door closed. "Have you not learned anything from the other day? It's not enough to be prejudiced against humans, you have to hate the twins too?"

"Fine, but when they murder me in my bed and fill my mouth with flowers, you'll know who to blame. And never call me Shottie again. It's a terrible nickname, and we're never going to be friends."

There's no point talking to her, so I walk back down the hallway. Part of me thinks I should stay back and make sure Deadshot doesn't do anything stupid, like try to murder *them* in their beds, but surely she wouldn't be that—

Deadshot pushes past me, and slams her way out of the house. When I peer out the window, she's sitting on the front step. It's about as far away as she can be and still count as 'helping' with the sitting job.

The next hour for the rest of us passes peacefully, and we end up making crepes. Once the final batch is done and steaming lightly on the table, I remember why we're actually here.

"We should check on the kids," I say. "They've been ominously quiet."

Cammie shakes her head. "They're sleeping. Take advantage of the fact and don't wake them up."

Dopple's brow crinkles. "Better safe than sorry with Biome's kids." A duplicate splits off and pads down the hallway. Obviously he wasn't sure. The original stands there and shrugs.

It's thirty seconds before we hear the scream.

The three of us bolt down the hallway. A few seconds later, the front door bangs as Deadshot joins us.

The Dopple duplicate is standing in the doorway.

Kel reaches him first. "What on earth are you shrieking about?"

He turns, and his gaze is horrified. "They're gone."

CHAPTER TWELVE

IN WHICH WE GO FOR A WALK AND I'M SURE EVERYTHING WILL TURN OUT FINE

"THEY CAN'T BE *GONE*." I push past Kel and into my room. It's exactly the same as when I left it, except for two important things.

The window is open.

And the children are definitely not here.

Then Kel disappears too, just a fading rainbow to show where she was.

I run over to the bed and prod it, as if I'll find them sunken into the moss. There are only indentations of where they'd been curled up. My eyes scan the room, but it's not like I live in a cluttered space. My closet is open and there's no sign of them inside. They can't have vanished, which leaves the window as the only obvious clue.

Deadshot looks bored, which is the worst reaction. "I told you they were pranking us."

"By running away?" Dopple's eyes are wild. He runs to the window and leans half his body out.

"These are Biome's kids," Cammie moans. "This is

going to look really bad on our record."

"No it won't, because they ran away." Deadshot leans against the wall with her arms folded. "They want all of us to be in trouble."

"If they were going to prank anyone, it would be you and you alone," I snap. I'm tired of her. "You're the only one they had a problem with, because you can't shut up with your bigoted nonsense. In fact—"

"There are wolf tracks here," Dopple says. "Outside the window. Massive paws leading away."

We all jostle for space to see what he's talking about, but they're obvious. They're pressed into the soft mud and look like a giant dog has been there.

I pull my head back inside, almost smacking it on the window frame. My heart is racing. "But what does this mean?"

Deadshot yawns. "So the brats can turn into wolves. It only proves my theory."

"They don't have powers." Cammie is still shaking. "They're not mutants. There's no way they can randomly turn into wolves."

"So where did the wolves come from?" Dopple squeaks.

"I don't know where they came from." Kel appears back in the room, breathing hard and trailing rainbow light. "I know where they went though. They left the island on the land bridge. I followed the tracks halfway to the mainland, but I figured I should come back first."

"What are we saying?" I stare from face to face. "That the plant kids were taken by wolves who've been lurking around the island, waiting for their moment?"

Deadshot snorts. "Or they ran away on wolves. Do you think *those kids* would let wolves kidnap them? Can wolves even kidnap people?"

"Uh, hello. What exactly is going on?" It's a new and familiar voice, but not one I need right now.

I tangle my hands in my hair and say a very bad word.

"Effie?" Airy says. "Why are you talking about wolves kidnapping people?"

Everyone starts talking at once, spouting their theories. It's impossible to understand until Hazel shows up and shouts at us all to be quiet. Then we go around one at a time and explain what's happening. By the end, *everyone* looks nervous and worried.

Airy fidgets with her braid. "So Biome's kids are missing, and we have no idea if they left under their own steam or were taken by wolves, or more likely, someone who can control wolves with their power."

"Ohh," Dopple says. "That does make more sense."

Hazel's fingers are twitching like she wants to draw her pistols from the air. "Okay, I need to call Dylan right away."

"No," both Kel and I blurt at once. "We need to fix this ourselves."

"Airy, this is a terrible idea." Hazel puts a hand on my sister's arm.

"I know, I know. Eff, this is ridiculous. We need to go straight to Chatterbox and Marvellous. They've got people who are actually good at this stuff. If they've run away, they'll get in trouble and if something really bad has happened, they'll be able to deal with it."

"And in the meantime, we get punished again." My voice is shaking. "Because we let the kids escape or be taken. They'll kick me out, because I'm not a mutant and—"

"I know Dylan," Hazel says, cutting off my babbling. "They'll understand. Much better to come to them and explain than go racing off on a crazy errand which might get you all in trouble."

"Let us try first," I plead. "If it doesn't work, we can go straight to Chatterbox. Airy, please. Let me prove myself. I'm not just a stupid baseline, I can actually do something." I hate that everyone's here to hear this, but I can't stop thinking about Cybele in the forest and how she denied me any chance at power. Maybe if I can prove myself like this, she'll take pity and relent.

"Maybe we can take a quick look," Airy says to Hazel. "They might be roaming and we don't want to raise the alarm for nothing."

"They do like to wander." Hazel's frown smooths out. "And I wouldn't put it past them to go off to the mainland while there's a land bridge. What the wolves have to do with it, I have no idea."

"So that's a yes?" I ask.

Kel's basically vibrating with anticipation. Both Dopple and Cammie look nervous, and Deadshot is very quiet, probably in the hope of not attracting any more attention from Hazel.

"For a very limited time," Hazel says sternly. "At the first sign of trouble or weirdness, we're coming back. Can we all agree to that?"

"Sure," I say. "I mean yes."

"Yes," Kel says.

Cammie flickers against the wall. "I'm in, too."

"I'm not even sure we should be going at all," is Dopple's contribution. "But I'll go if everyone else is going."

"One of you can always stay behind," Kel smirks.

"What about you, Deadshot?" Hazel asks.

"I'm not coming. You do what you want."

"Okay, that works." Hazel nods. "You can let people know what's happened if they show up looking."

Deadshot's eyes flicker. "You mean if Biome turns up, I'm the one who has to explain everything?"

Airy and Hazel both grin. Kel does too.

"Fine, I'll come on this pointless errand. If we find these kids, they better give us enough credit to stop this babysitting nonsense."

"Aren't you just the most charming creature?" Airy looks at Deadshot with an expression I haven't seen from her in a while. "I'd be a lot more civil if you want me to forget what you did to my little sib."

"Bite me, mermaid," Deadshot says. "I'm not scared of any of you. Not even your bestie and her pathetic nightmare gun."

"Let's use her as bait for the wolves." Kel slings an arm around Deadshot's shoulder, like she usually does to me, but it's shrugged rudely off.

"Enough." Airy sounds much sharper and more grown up than usual. "If we're going to do this, you all need to follow and do what you're told. If you can't even do *that*, Deadshot, we'll shoot you with Dream and you can happily snooze the day away until Biome gets here."

Deadshot's cheeks flush again. For a second I almost feel sorry for her, even though it's her own fault for always being angry and rude. I know she doesn't like us, but it would be easier if she didn't make it so obvious.

Dopple stares out the window. "So should we follow the wolves, or search the island?"

"The wolves seem the obvious lead," Hazel says. "And it would be very on brand for the twins to ride wolves into the human world. They don't think like other people."

"We noticed," Kel says. "Weird kids, and that's coming from me."

We all climb out the window one at a time until we're standing in the small garden at the side of the house. I crouch down and press my fingers into the wolf prints. They're deep enough to make me think about how heavy the beasts must be.

Kel's trying to pace out the length of the wolf's stride, and she has to leap from print to print.

"Big wolves," Dopple says.

"Very." Hazel's lips purse. "Probably why the twins decided to ride them."

From here, it's about half an hour's walk to the land bridge, a raised platform of rocks and sand that runs in a gently winding path from the beach on the western tip of the island towards the bustling dock in the distance. I hadn't realised we'd gotten so close to land. Mutopia moves around a lot and spends most of its time far from other countries, but every so often it docks close to a country. Usually it's the cause for a whole series of excursions, so either this is brand new, or it's being kept secret for mysterious reasons.

"Let's go." Hazel strides off, like she's desperate to get this over with.

Airy shucks off her top and dives into the water, swimming alongside us with powerful strokes. She dives down under the water until we can't see her and pops up in front of us, spouting water into the air like she's a whale.

"Show-off," I mutter. It's not entirely fair because if she's not in water enough, she starts to dry out and it can actually get really bad. She hasn't had a serious attack in a long time. The last one was one of the scariest experiences of the Dark Year. I remember dragging her out of the walls while she convulsed, holding her face under the kitchen tap. Water dripped down her parched throat, glistening against her skin as her gills fluttered.

The whole time we could hear the soldiers going door to door on the floor below. We resuscitated her enough to keep her alive, and got her back behind the walls just in time. When the soldiers reached our apartment, I explained away the water as accidental flooding. They searched and shouted and waved guns in my face, but they didn't discover the secret entrance.

It gives me a surge of warmth to see Airy frolicking in the water now. Everything in the Dark Year was worth it now that we've found somewhere where my sister is safe.

It takes us almost an hour to reach the end of the land bridge. Kel's complaining about the slowness has reached the point where I'm pretty sure Airy is ready to drown her, and Deadshot is breathing with exaggerated patience.

"We're not splitting up," Hazel says with impressive calm. "I've told you this, Kel."

"Send her back," Deadshot growls. "It's like having a nagging child ask if we're there yet."

"My point is that I *could have* been there and back like fifty times," Kel sighs.

"Which would involve splitting up, which we're not doing." Hazel's lip twitches.

"I can push her in for you," I offer.

"We're almost there anyway," Hazel says, and she's correct. We're walking among ships of all different sizes that bob restlessly in the ocean. They're named things like *Waterlily* and *Wavejumper* and *Lazy Line Painter Jane*. None of them seem to be occupied and they drift under the overcast sky. In the distance, larger ships are moored, nosed up against giant warehouses. These ones bustle with people, shouting to each other over the faint grind of machinery.

Finally the land bridge reaches the edge of the docks. Hazel stands with hands on hips. "So here's the problem. Wolves don't leave footprints on wood."

Airy hauls herself dripping from the sea and wicks the water from her clothes. "We could ask if anyone's seen giant wolves roaming around."

"Or we follow that." Dopple points to one of the

bollards which has a series of long grey hairs on it. "Turns out wolves shed."

"Suspicious," Hazel mutters. "Like a trail left for us to follow."

"It doesn't feel good." Airy squints into the distance. "You think we should go back?"

Hazel glances over her shoulder at the land bridge we've just traversed. "We've come all this way, so let's poke around a little more. Maybe it'll be wolves shedding after all. Do they shake themselves like dogs when they've been wet?"

Nobody knows the answer to this, not even Dopple, so we head off down the dock. We follow this around for a while until we hit land, where we rediscover the faint outlines of sandy wolf-prints.

"Yes!" Kel's about to go sprinting off, but Hazel grabs her just in time, skidding along for a few rainbow-tinged paces.

"Stick *together*, Kel," I mutter.

The path heads towards a series of low buildings, and forms an alleyway between two of them. We enter with Hazel in the lead. At the end, the slim figure of a boy leans against one of the walls.

"Hi there," Hazel calls. "Have you seen any wolves around?"

The boy springs upright and points at us. "Finally. I thought you'd never get here."

"What are you talking about?" Deadshot asks.

"Keep up." The boy puts his hands in his pockets and grins. "We've been waiting for you. This is one of those things. What do you call it? Oh, yeah. A trap."

CHAPTER THIRTEEN

TRAP IS A FOUR LETTER WORD

"KEL," Hazel snaps.

For once in her life Kel doesn't question but speeds past me, heading back down the alleyway. I'm still staring at this boy in front of us, but when there's a massive thump, I turn to see Kel sprawled on the ground. A second Dopple runs helter-skelter past her and smacks into an invisible barrier. He bounces off it with a cry, pressing his hand to his face. I can't even *see* Cammie, and I assume she's vanished but I've no idea *where*.

I run for Kel. She hit the invisible wall at speed, so the impact must have been terrible. She's out cold but her chest is still rising and falling.

Hazel joins me, pressing her fingertips to Kel's neck. "God, I hope she's okay."

Deadshot crouches and picks up a stone from the ground. Without even looking, she whips it towards the boy, who's still grinning at us from the end of the alley.

The stone ricochets off another invisible barrier right in front of his smug face and flies back to hit Deadshot in the shoulder. She lets out a whole string of swear words.

"Trapped all around." Airy shivers. "In some kind of bubble."

"Yes, we figured that out, fish girl," Deadshot sneers.

"The question is why." Hazel's still crouched by Kel, stroking her forehead. "He's obviously a mutant so why lure us into—"

"Because we caught the wrong mutants." A second figure joins the boy on the other side of the forcefield—a very tall woman with pale skin. She's flanked on each side by two enormous grey wolves with big snouts, lolling tongues and bright green eyes.

"You wanted Biome," Hazel says.

"We did *expressly* lure their children away in their expectation the parents would come a-running. Remarkably disappointing to find a rag-tag group like you, but I suppose we must make do with what we have."

Hazel's back on her feet. She flexes her fingers, and Dream and Nightmare appear in her hands. This close, I can feel the chill from the black and silver gun.

"They're going to drop the barrier and attack. Be ready. Protect Kel if you can. And Deadshot?"

"On it." Deadshot restlessly juggles a handful of stones. "Bet you're glad you nagged me into coming now, aren't you?"

This seems like a wild rewriting of what happened,

but my heart is knocking so painfully in my chest that I can't speak. This is going to be one of those mutant battles I've read about. The ones from stories. And here I am, in the middle of it, all because I was too stubborn. Some pitiful human bystander about to be—

I OPEN my eyes to find myself in a small stone room. The walls are rough. The roof looks the same.

I'm completely alone.

My brain has no recollection of how I got here. Last I remember we were in the alley, surrounded by the forcefield, with Hazel and the others preparing to fight.

I guess we lost.

I'm lying in a bed, although it's uncomfortable with a single thin blanket over a foam mattress. There's no pillow. The only other furniture is a steel toilet and a bucket of water. There's a single window high up on one wall and a wooden door with a glass pane.

"A cell." My voice sounds croaky and small. "It's not a room at all."

When I swing my feet off the bed and stand up, I'm slightly dizzy but nothing hurts. I prod my head and stomach and various other places, but there are no sore spots. However they knocked me out, it didn't leave any marks. Probably someone's mutant power.

And now I'm trapped, with no idea of where Willow and Soo-yeon are. We're literally the worst babysitters *ever*. Biome will be furious, and fair enough too.

"Think, Effie," I say. I'm not sure why being alone makes me talk to myself, but it does. It helps a lot when I'm anxious. Back during the Dark Year, I'd talk to myself during my journeys into the city. "Effie awoke to find themself in a cell. They desperately needed to pee, which was gross because there was only a single battered metal toilet to use for that purpose."

I don't bother narrating the next part, but it does make me feel a little better.

"They crossed to the small window in the cell door and looked out. Across from them was an identical door, but nobody stood at it. Were they alone? Were the children okay, and what was the fate of their friends? Did anybody know they were gone? What was the chance of rescue?"

The problem with being my own narrator is that I have no answers to any of these questions. A narrator gets to see the story from outside, whereas I'm stuck in my own head, limited by my own perspective.

If I had *anything* at all useful, I could try picking the lock. My hair's too short for hairpins, and I wouldn't even know where to start even if I had one. Instead, I give the door a series of hard thumps. It's very solid, but at least it makes a noise. There's silence in response, but I bang again, because there's nothing else to do.

Finally, I hear a faint answering bang. Success!

I beat out a rhythmic pattern and then wait for the echoed response.

I try a different pattern, and this time I get two echoes. Definitely other people in here with me. I've got to assume it's my friends. There's a whole bunch of banging now, coming from all sides, too much to distinguish individual patterns, like we're all slamming mindlessly on the door just to be heard.

Then a head appears at the window of the cell opposite mine. Scruffy hair and tan skin and a wide smile.

Kel.

She's standing and alive and doesn't look the worse for wear at all. She waves at me, like we've ended up surprise bunkmates at a summer camp.

Tears flood my eyes. She mimes tears trailing down her cheeks and then sucking her thumb like a baby. I make a rude gesture back and she staggers backwards as if she's been shot. Then I make a little heart with my fingers and she gives me one in return.

She's okay. That's a good sign.

It's a pretty weird definition of okay, given that we're all trapped in cells by mysterious mutants who caught us in a trap meant for Biome, but at least we're alive and breathing.

The banging falls silent as people realise it's not actually doing anything. I wish I knew Morse Code. I don't know any way to say "Hi, it's me, Effie. I'm fine. How is everyone else?"

There are a few more bangs from somewhere, presumably someone who hasn't realised the pointlessness of it yet. If I had to guess, it's Deadshot.

Kel and I make helpless gestures at each other. Kel rubs her head and mimes being sore.

I hold up one hand like a wall and waggle two

fingers like running feet, moving them so they smack into the wall and bounce off.

Kel rubs her head again and mimes crying.

I try and mime *children* by making two people with my fingers, one a lot smaller than the other. Kel looks very confused. I flail my arms like the plant kids too, but she only pinwheels her own arms in response.

"Where are the kids, Kel?" I shout.

She shouts something back at me, but the sound is too muffled.

I twist one finger and against my flat palm, which is supposed to mean *key*.

Kel shrugs and looks at me like I'm crazy. I try a few more times, but her expressions of confusion get increasingly theatrical. It's a waste of time anyway. If Kel had a key, we'd be out of here. My shoulders slump, and I'm about to turn away when—

Another face appears outside my door. Looking directly in at me. The face disappears, and a piece of paper is held up to the window. STAND BACK is written in rough capitals.

I don't do what I'm told. I don't see the point. The paper is removed, and I try to peer sideways to see whoever put it there, but there's no sign of them. Kel is making gestures at me, but I can't understand any of them.

A new piece of paper is slapped on the door. STAND BACK OR STAY IN THERE. YOUR CALL.

I sigh, even though nobody can hear me, and walk backwards until I'm pressed up against the far wall of the cell. "Effie realised they had no choice. They may as well learn something about their captors."

The door opens, and the boy from the alleyway steps inside.

"No trouble, okay? Else I'll stick you in a bubble and leave you for my sister."

I don't even know who his sister is. Wolf Lady seemed way too old. Either way, there isn't much I can do with all my no-powers except to go along with it.

"Sure, no trouble. What are we doing?"

"You're coming to talk to the boss lady." He grins at me. For a kidnapper, he's got a nice smile. "Don't worry. The wolves don't bite and she barely does."

"Fine." I push myself off the wall. "Lead the way."

"No funny business. First sign of trouble and zap." He waggles his fingers at me.

"I'm shaking, I'm shaking." I walk towards him and he scuttles out of the room.

"Follow me. Don't touch anything, don't signal to your friends."

Kel gives me a little wave and I give her an eyebrow arch back. Outside the cell door is a long passageway of identical rooms. Kel and I are at one end, but unfortunately we turn right, leading away from the other cells. I want to see who's here and how they're doing. If Airy's in here and doesn't have enough water…

Part of me wants to run back and see what *zap* means, but I can probably guess. Instead, I trot along dutifully after the boy. There's a short corridor and then a long staircase going down. At the bottom of each flight, the boy checks over his shoulder.

"You look nervous," he says when we reach the bottom. We've come out into yet another stone corridor. There are no windows, only old-fashioned torches set in brackets on the wall. I think we're locked in some ancient castle, and I wonder where in the world we are.

"Why would I be nervous? I've only been knocked out, kidnapped and locked up. That happens to me every day."

"You're a funny boy," he says.

"I'm not a boy." I stand still and glare at him.

"Sorry." He gestures. "Really, I am. It's just with the hair and, well, I don't actually know."

"I'm not a girl either. I'm in between."

Now he's frowning. "How does that work?"

"It doesn't *work* like anything. I'm just not a boy or a girl. I'm something else."

"Huh," he says. "You're kinda pretty either way."

"Shut up." I give him my best sneer, modelled after Deadshot. "You can't tell the person you kidnapped that they're pretty. It's creepy."

"Sorry. Wow, feels like I'm setting some world record for apologies."

"You haven't apologised for kidnapping me yet, so you've still got a way to go."

This makes him laugh, and that's nice too. I hate that I notice it, but I do. "It's not my idea to kidnap you. I'm a lowly hench. Me and my sister both are."

"What's a hench?" I ask.

"Can we walk and talk at the same time, please?" He gestures in a come-along motion, and starts walking again. "A hench is someone who does work for, like, a villain or someone more important."

"So you know your boss is a bad guy?" I'd been holding a slender hope this boy stumbled into his life of crime by accident. "A *kidnapper*. You better hope the kids are okay. Otherwise you're in big, big trouble. Being a hench isn't going to get you a free pass."

His expression darkens, all the sweetness gone in an instant. "Not everyone gets a pretty life on Mutopia." We've reached a set of huge wooden double doors. The hinges are black iron and there are big metal rings for handles. He braces himself against the left door and shoves it open. "Here we are. The villain of the story."

CHAPTER FOURTEEN

OH GREAT! NOW THERE'S A VILLAIN! COULD THINGS BE ANY WORSE?

THE ROOM REVEALED behind the doors has seen better days, but must have been grand once upon a time. The ceiling soars overhead, and there are big floor-to-ceiling stained glass windows that let in coloured light. Most of the furniture is pushed into haphazard piles in the corner, except for one tall wooden seat, carved with a complex pattern of stars and circles. It's very much got throne vibes.

Seated at the foot of it are the two wolves, curled nose to tail with each other. It reminds me of how the plant kids slept. There's still no sign of Willow and Soo-yeon at all, which is a very big problem. We were supposed to be looking after them. It's our whole job! And now they're who knows where.

The only other person in the room with us is the woman from before. Somehow, seated in the chair, she's even more intimidating. She's changed into a dress of black and red that clings tight to her body and then flares out around her legs like a bloody ocean in the darkness. Her hair is pinned up into a tower on her head, kept in place by silver pins with snarling wolf snouts. It's her green eyes that are most arresting, large and beautiful, with almost no white.

She leans forward. "Greetings. My name is Lupine. I'm intrigued to meet the mystery at last."

"Mystery?" I'm so confused.

"Yes. We've been unable to determine your power. There's the one who likes to throw things, and the poor confused duplicator. Then there's the fast one, and isn't she a handful? And the older two—the mermaid and the one with the guns who's caused me no end of sleep problems. And you, who everyone is very closed-mouthed about. Did you pry any information out of her on the way down, Wally?"

"They're not a boy or a girl," the boy says. I don't like the name Wally, and not just because its a stupid pun. With the way he looks, he deserves something autumnal and pretty. That's an embarrassing thought. I hope none of them are mind readers. And wait—did she miss mentioning Cammie on purpose or accidentally?

The woman waves one hand as if my gender or lack of it is unimportant. "You're here to explain your powers. I doubt you have anything particularly useful, or you'd have broken out already."

I say nothing, because otherwise I'll start laughing. My mysterious power is being the most ordinary person on the island. Better keep my secret locked up tight.

"Hmm." The woman peers at me. "Perhaps you're

probing for information even now. Using some form of psychic ability? I suppose it doesn't matter, as long as you remain within our grasp."

Wally shoots me a glance, but I carry on saying nothing, because it seems safest.

The woman shifts irritably in her throne. "Tell me—how close are you to the entity known as Biome?"

I frown. "You mean Chatterbox and Marvellous? There are two of them. They're not a single entity."

She arches one eyebrow at me. "I think you'll find your two former mutant heroes are more closely linked than you believe. They may be differentiated in physical form, but psychically they are connected through an immensely powerful energy matrix." She sighs. "I did *so* want to meet them."

I clench my jaw. Anger and worry war in my stomach, making it ache. "Don't worry. They'll come for you. You took their *kids*. Then you'll wish you hadn't met them."

She smirks a little at this, just a tweak of her mouth. "I am hardly that foolish. They were supposed to stumble into this trap mostly unawares, as you did. Now they'll be forewarned so we'll have to be even more subtle." She sits her elbow on her knee and her chin on her hand to regard me closely. "Which takes us back to the question of your mysterious powers."

I'd love to pretend to have cool powers, but it's not the sort of thing you can fake. It's best to stall instead, and hope someone with *real* cool powers can do something to help me.

"It's a huge surprise," I say.

"So dramatic," the lady says with an eye roll. "Isn't this one cute, Wally? Shall we get Flicker in here to encourage this one to talk?"

"Just tell her." The boy stares at me, shuffling from foot to foot. "It's much easier that way. For everyone."

Lupine smiles, and she looks a little like a wolf herself. "Yes. That way, I don't have to watch while you twitch and wet yourself. Flicker gets a rest, and Wally doesn't have to sulk in his room about all the evil I make him do."

I don't like the sound of this at all. Besides, it's not like my secret is amazing or anything.

"I'm a baseline," I say, fast like I'm ripping a bandaid off. "Just a plain old boring human. No powers at all."

"No," the woman says in disbelief.

I shrug. "My sister has water manipulation powers, one of my Dads has cooking powers and one can mould wood. They all got changed at once and I was skipped."

Lupine laughs, high and delighted. "A human. Not an unpleasant surprise, but rather dull."

It's not like I don't already know this. I stare back at her as if all her words mean nothing. While I'm here, there's stuff that *I* want to find out. "Are the kids okay?"

"The little monsters live." Lupine looks down her nose at me. "I would hardly hurt my bargaining chips now, would I? We'll find some other way to lure their parents in, never fear." She pulls one of the silver pins from her hair and twirls in between her fingers. The two wolves sit up, their unnatural green-eyed attention all focused on me.

All the other emotions in my stomach fall away, leaving only fear. I take a shaky step backwards.

"No, little human." Lupine waves her hand, as if she's brushing me aside. Now that I'm human, I don't even register. "I am not that much of a monster. Murder of someone pointless like you serves me no purpose. Wally, take them back to their cell. I shall walk with the wolves and see if any ideas manifest themselves."

She gets up in a single movement. I cringe away from her because she's so imposing.

"What are your powers?" I ask croakily.

"Here's a hint." She winks at me. "It's not the wolves."

Wally takes me gently by the arm and leads me out of the room. He's a lot less smiley and talkative as we walk down the corridors. In fact, he doesn't say a word until we reach the stairs. "She's lying. Her power isn't *only* the wolves. She has control over many animals, but they're her favourites." He swallows hard. "She can place part of her mind inside them, so when they roam, she sees what they do."

"She sent them off to Mutopia, to lure the twins?" I ask. We've reached the top of the stairs, and we pause at the door to my cell as he unlocks it.

"Yes," he says. "But not only them. Now get inside and be sensible."

I catch a glimpse of Kel, who gives me an expression of exaggerated surprise and question. There's nothing to report—at least nothing I can say in charades—so all I do is shrug.

The door slams behind me, and I hear the key turn. I return to the window to look at Kel. Communication is too difficult—if only we'd learned sign language—and we end up pulling faces at each other until that gets boring too.

Kel's the one who sits down first, and I go back to my bed and stare at the ceiling. It feels a lot less comfortable now that I know what's going on. My brain goes back over what Lupine said. This is all about Biome. She wants to get hold of them and possibly the energy matrix? I think that must be something to do with Cybele. It seems like a very dangerous plan, but she is a villain after all. The problem is we're all trapped here and I don't really know what we can do about it. We need to get out and save Willow and Sooyeon, but we're all separated. It's incredibly frustrating but—

There's a click from the door, and I lift my head up. How is Wally back *already*?

It opens very slowly, someone ensuring it doesn't make a sound. I scramble off the bed, but there's nobody there. At least nobody that's visible.

The faint outline of a person appears, framed against the door.

"Effie," the outline whispers. "It's me."

I bite back a laugh of glee and throw myself at her. It's a weird feeling, hugging a barely visible person, but she feels as warm and real as ever. "Cammie! How did you—?"

"I went invisible at the start, and I don't think they ever saw me. It was really hard to watch, but the wolves and the girl who could zap people, it seemed like the safest thing. They took you all away, but I rode on top of their jeep."

"Wow, I can't believe how brave you were." I'm still clinging to her and she doesn't seem to mind.

"I wasn't brave." She doesn't pull away, but I feel wetness on her cheeks. "I hid, Effie."

"Sometimes that's the best thing you can do." I pat her hair awkwardly. "Are you okay?"

"Sort of. I've been trying to find a way to get you out. I stole your key from that boy when he came down the stairs. But we'd better hurry and get out of here before he notices."

"What about the others?" I ask.

"The keys are all different." Cammie's mostly visible now, and she crosses to Kel's cell to show me how the key won't even fit. "We'll have to come back. Effie, please. If we wait too long, they'll catch us."

"Do you know where Willow and Soo-yeon are?" I ask.

"I'll tell you everything once we're *safe*." Cammie's voice is much more stern than usual.

I cast another look at Kel's face up close to the cell window. It feels terrible leaving her there, and I haven't had a chance to even look at the others yet, but Cammie's already towing me towards the stairs. Part of me wants to argue, but she's the one who's been brave and done the rescue, so I need to trust her.

We're about halfway down when we hear footsteps

from below. Oh yikes. I guess Cammie was right about hurrying. We're trapped in the stairwell with nowhere to go but up. Cammie immediately blends into the stone.

"That's not going to work for me," I hiss.

"Where is it, where is it?"

She's invisible, so I can't see what she's doing. In the meantime, I'm standing on the stairs, ready to be caught. At least if they find an empty cell, it'll be a *mystery*.

I'm on the verge of running back to my cell, when there's a grinding sound. A section of the wall slides inwards, revealing pitch-black darkness. "Remember four-eighteen," Cammie whispers, and tugs me into the darkness.

We're inside a very narrow passageway, pressed up against the stone walls. Cammie reaches past me and presses something which causes the hidden door to slide back into place. All the light is extinguished and I can't see a single thing. I'm about to say something, but Cammie puts her hand over my mouth. Her lips are pressed up against my ear. "Trust me."

From behind the stone wall, sound is muffled but we hear footsteps and whistling. It sounds like Wally. We wait for him to go past without speaking.

"They'll find you missing soon and sound the alarm." Cammie's mouth tickles my ear. "We can't risk the stairs. We'll have to stay here for a while. They'll search the castle, but they won't find us."

I press my own face against her ear. Her skin is really warm. "Are you sure?"

"They haven't caught me yet." Her lips brush my neck and it makes me shiver.

"What about the kids?"

"They're nowhere in the main castle, but there's a tower out in the grounds. I've tried to reach it, but there's the wolves." She shivers. "They catch my scent even when I'm invisible, and I have to lose them in the gross old tunnels."

"Take me to the tower." My voice sounds far more sure than I really am.

"Effie, we *can't*. Those wolves will kill us."

"We're the Mutantsitters Club. If we're too scared to look after those kids, what good are we?"

"Alive to come up with a better plan."

I can't argue with the not being eaten by wolves part, but we do need *some* kind of plan.

"Now come with me and be careful. We'll go nice and slow." Cammie threads her fingers through mine and we edge our way through the tunnel. I use my other hand to feel the wall in front of me, so I don't accidentally bump myself.

A short time later, there's some light up ahead, and as it gets brighter I realise it's coming from a hole in the ground.

"Home sweet home," Cammie says in a normal voice. "It's not much, but it's safe." She crouches down and shimmies through the hole, holding onto the edge and dropping down safely.

"Where are we?" I ask.

"I think it's a little safe room where people could hide from invaders. It's at the center of a few secret passages, like they wanted to be able to access it from different parts of the castle. Come on, Eff. It's perfectly safe."

I lower myself down in the same way that Cammie did. The chamber we're in is perfectly circular, with no windows. A couple of the stones in the walls have been marked with x's, presumably to show how to open secret exits. There's no furniture aside from a pile of blankets and a couple of buckets.

"Clean water," Cammie says. "To use the bathroom I usually just sneak into the east wing where nobody's staying. The wolves almost caught me in there once though, so you have to be careful."

"I've been recently." I blush.

"That's good. One less thing to worry about." She yawns enormously, covering it with one hand. "Sorry, I'm exhausted. I want to come up with a real plan, but I should probably sleep first."

I pat her shoulder awkwardly. "It's fine. Take your chance to sleep. I can keep watch."

Cammie fidgets and stares at the blankets. "It's the sleep part that scares me."

"Of falling asleep?" I'm confused. "Why?"

She shakes her head. "Of dreaming."

CHAPTER FIFTEEN

SWEET DREAMS ARE MADE OF... LOTS OF WEIRD THINGS

I'M STARING AT CAMMIE, all confused. "I don't understand. You're having nightmares?"

Her hands fidget among the pile of blankets, smoothing and crumpling. "Have you not slept since you've been here?"

"I woke up a few hours before you came to find me. The last thing I remember before *that* was being in the alleyway and Kel getting hurt."

Cammie's eyes go all big. "That was nearly two days ago."

"I slept for two days?" This worries me more than anything. What's been happening? The kids who we're supposed to be babysitting have been locked in some tower this whole time!

"Yeah, I think that zappy girl hit everyone differently. Deadshot and Kel bounced back pretty quick, but Dopple only just woke up too."

"Nobody's come to rescue us." My stomach is queasy. "*Or* the plant kids. Which means..."

Cammie stares at me, waiting for me to finish. "It means what?"

"They can't *find* us. Biome, I mean. Otherwise they'd be here, wouldn't they? Doing the big rescue."

Cammie looks at the floor. "It's bad, I know."

I close my eyes, wishing I could go somewhere else, but it only leaves me in the dark. Everything is terrible and we're lost with nobody coming to save us. "And the others? Are they all okay? Even Airy?"

"I think so. I've been checking on them every day and communicating through the doors. Lupine only talks to them one at a time. Everyone's tried to escape, but Wally puts them in a bubble and then Flicker zaps them."

"I didn't try to escape," I say with a sigh.

"You don't have powers." Cammie pats my shoulder and yawns again, finishing with a shiver.

"What's so scary about dreaming?" I ask.

She shakes her head instead of answering.

"Fine, I'll sleep too." I collapse down onto the pile of blankets and curl up. It's far from the best bed I've ever slept on.

Cammie joins me on the blankets, finding her own little spot. She rolls over and closes her eyes. Within a few seconds, a whimper escapes her lips.

"What's wrong?"

"Last time I slept..." There's a long enough pause that I think she might have fallen asleep again. "Can you move closer to me?"

"Uh, yeah, sure." I wriggle over, towing my blanket with me and lie so my back is pressed up against hers.

Cammie stays that way for a moment and then rolls over. Her hand touches me and then withdraws.

"Is it okay if I put my arm around you?"

I take her hand in mine and pull her arm across me. She nestles in closer, and I can feel her warmth all up and down my body. My heart is thumping in my chest and I'm not sure exactly why.

"Cammie?" I whisper.

She doesn't answer, and her breathing is soft and even. Her hand nestles in mine. She's safe with me and has no need to hide.

I close my eyes, certain sleep won't claim me.

WHEN I OPEN THEM AGAIN, I'm lying in water a few inches deep. Hazel sits in an enormous armchair nearby, wearing an unlikely combination of a bikini and a trenchcoat. She has a choker around her neck with gold and silver skulls on it.

"Um. Hi." I get to my feet, dripping water everywhere. It rolls away downhill as if I'm standing on a slope, but the ground looks perfectly flat.

"Effie, finally! What do you see me as?"

"Um, you in a, well, in a, uh, bathing costume and a coat."

"Oh thank god." She stands up and tugs the coat around herself. "Everyone else sees a terrifying monster and blunders away into horrible dreams."

"You look normal to me." I splash over to her. "What about the plant kids? Do *you* know where they are? Cammie says—"

"I've seen their dreams." Hazel frowns. "Sort of. Every time I try to reach them, I get stuck in the forest. There's a massive treehouse covered in thorns with a sign that says *no non-plants allowed.*"

Relief floods through me like an ocean. "So they're okay, but we need to find them."

"It'll be a lot easier once we get out of these cells." Hazel scowls. "Which is step one of my plan."

"What's step two?"

She grins at me. "Step two is a bunch of question marks. Step three—rescue the kids."

I don't have a better plan, and *rescue kids* is the main thing we need to worry about. I look down at my wet feet. "Why is there water everywhere?"

"It's leaking over from Airy's dreams, which is…" She gestures around herself wildly. "Probably my other biggest worry at the moment. I'll show you in a second. I got a little too trigger-happy with Nightmare when we got captured, and I think everyone's catching them like a disease. So when I try to rally people for an escape, they all flee in horror. So much fun." She brightens a little. "Still, at least you can see me, so maybe you can translate."

"You said something about Airy?" I feel light-headed.

"It's easier if I show you, and then we can figure out what to do."

"You're not making me feel any better." My voice is getting high and hysterical. "Everyone's trapped in cells, and the plant kids are locked up *somewhere* and—"

"Effie, don't freak out." Hazel links her arm through mine. "There's a plan, remember? Now don't let go, because this is going to get weird." She looks around in frustration at the endless expanse of ocean. "It's such a pain finding *doors* in some of these places."

"Is this normal?" I ask. "I mean, do you usually show up in people's dreams?"

"No, but only because it's incredibly rude. I visit Airy a lot since I have an open invitation. Other people, no way." She shudders. "You see things you don't want to see. But right now we have to take drastic measures."

"And this is *my* dream?"

"Yes, but if we want to get into someone else's we're going to need a door."

There are definitely no doors around. It's all just ocean, with no sign of land. The water is very clear, with tiny orange fish swimming around my bare feet. It's the same in every direction, which means we'll have to walk for miles. It's not even as if there's—

"You're a natural," Hazel says.

A ship floats in the ocean in front of us, boards creaking and waves lapping against its sides. It's got billowing white sails and three masts. The middle one flies a flag with a rainbow-coloured skull. Attached to the bow is an incredibly detailed figure made of wood that looks remarkably like Ms. Sefo. The figurehead turns her head to look at us, blinking.

"Effie and Hazel. You're dreadfully discombobu-lated. Standing around in all this jello as if you're late for the party."

"It's not jello," I protest, but when I look down again, I'm standing in mounds of blue and green. The fish in it are made of gummy candy and are motionless.

"No, of course not, dear. Denying physical reality is always the best course of action when confronted with the impossible. Now why don't you climb aboard and get out of those wet clothes." She winks at me, and a ladder drops from the side of the boat.

"Up you go," Hazel mutters. "There's bound to be a door on board and we can get away from your weird fascination with your teacher. This is why I don't like being in other people's dreams."

Blushing, I scramble up the ladder at the side of the ship. My feet skid a little on the rungs and I realise they're made of slightly melting chocolate. My finger-tips are covered with it, and I suck one experimentally.

"Don't eat the boat," Hazel calls from behind me. "If you sink it, who knows what's next?"

I resist temptation and make it up to the deck, where there's a circular door into a cabin off to the right.

"You really are good at this." Hazel strides for the door, and I stumble along in her wake. She kicks it open with one foot. It's like opening an airlock in a space movie, or falling into a giant vacuum cleaner. We're both sucked helplessly in.

I give a tiny squawk, but the instant we're through, the sensation is gone. We're standing in a quiet and carefully manicured garden. The entrance to an enormous and complicated hedge maze is nearby, overgrown with flowers. Butterflies flicker through the air like fluttering shreds of colour. There's a tall, spreading oak tree nearby. My attention is drawn to the two figures sitting on a blanket spread under the tree.

One is a girl of fourteen, in a yellow dress that glows against her skin, and dark eyes that sparkle as she pours lemonade from an ornate jug with a wolf's head painted on it. The other, lying sprawled beside her, has dark hair that curls at the temples and neck, and blue eyes that watch every movement the girl makes.

I recognise the girl instantly as Cammie, but it takes me a while to realise the other person is me. How are there two of me here?

"Shhh," Hazel murmurs.

"Don't say a word." Cammie hands dream-me a glass of lemonade. "Do you feel it watching?"

Dream-Effie starts to turn, but Cammie draws their face back towards her.

"It's out there." She whispers it, but her voice reaches us clearly. "An invisible shadow. It blends into the world, just like me, but you can always see its eyes. They're burning holes cut through the wall to hell."

"What does it want?" Dream-Effie's voice shakes.

"What all monsters want." Cammie blinks her enormous eyes at me. "To eat."

"The door's probably in the maze." Hazel tugs at my hand. "Walk very quietly and slowly in that direction. If they notice us, Cammie's bound to start screaming. She thinks I'm the monster."

It's hard to look away from the pair under the tree. They look so happy together. I realise with a jolt that we're also lying tangled up together in a mess of blankets in the real world. The way dream-me looks at Cammie makes my heart beat faster and sweat prickle on the back of my neck.

"It's a dream." Hazel grips my hand tight as we sidle towards the opening of the maze, which looks increasingly like a mouth made to devour us. "Don't look at them."

I force my eyes away from the scene, but the instant I do there's a high-pitched scream.

"There," Cammie shouts. "Do you see it? It's followed us!"

They're both staring at Hazel and me. I wonder what they see.

"Leave it," dream-Effie hisses. "You need to get away from the monster. It wants your soul."

"How do you know?" Cassie's eyes fill with tears.

"Can't you hear it?"

"I don't want to." She gets to her feet, hands clapped to the sides of her head, and dashes towards the hedge maze. Dream-Effie follows, almost tripping over their feet as they disappear into the yawning opening.

"God, going in there after them is only going to make it worse," Hazel says.

"No need." I point at the tree where they'd been

sitting. Set neatly into it is a small wooden door painted red. There are words printed faintly on it, impossible to make out fully.

Hazel gives me an impressed nod. "You're *very* good at this."

We run and pull the door open. Despite how small it is, there's the same sensation of gravity inverting to pull us in. We fall through together and...

We're standing in a big room like a school gymnasium. A long row of targets is set up at one end. Near us on the wall is a pair of double doors that are still swinging as if someone just shoved their way through them.

"Let's head over there, nice and easy," Hazel says, but my attention is caught by something else.

Standing near us, Kel holds a bow and arrow almost as tall as she is, facing the row of targets at the end with an intent look on face. Beside her is Deadshot, standing very, very close.

"Relax this arm," Deadshot says, her fingers against Kel's bare skin. "And raise this one a little." Her other arm reaches around Kel's body, making minute adjustments to her stance. They're frozen like that, until Kel's face turns and is almost touching Deadshot's.

"Is this right?"

"Whose dream is this?" I ask Hazel.

"Not sure. There's no time to figure it out. And besides, it's rude to spy." She tows me, protesting, in the direction of the door. As we walk, a million balloons descend from the ceiling and obscure the others from view. I'm not sure whether I'm relieved or disappointed.

We hit the doors at a run and barely even feel the tugging sensation as they swing open.

Instead, we plunge headfirst into water again.

CHAPTER SIXTEEN

WHY IS IT THAT PLAN SHAPED THINGS ARE ALWAYS SO TERRIFYING?

WATER, water everywhere. I flail around in it, desperately looking for the surface. There's nothing but the same cool blue in every direction, not even any difference in the light. This is really not good.

Something grabs my leg and I scream. The sound comes out just fine, despite being underwater. I struggle free, but then I notice the creature that's gotten hold of me is Hazel. She swims up so we're floating side by side in the water. "Are you good now?"

"You could have warned me!"

"I thought you might recognise your sister's dream."

"Airy? Is she okay? Where is she, anyway?"

Hazel frowns. "Usually she finds me straight away, but things have been getting weirder lately. The space between things is bigger. It's part of the reason I'm so worried. She gets lost here."

"What does that mean? It's just a dream." I spin in

a slow circle. Now I spy a darkness in the distance, a drifting cloud that hangs in the water. "Is that her?"

"I hope not." Hazel's eyes are worried. "If it is…"

I don't wait for her to finish the sentence, but start thrashing through the water. I'm not actually that good a swimmer, despite growing up with a sister who's a mermaid. Usually I'd hold onto her and be pulled through the water, so I never really needed to learn properly. She's so free under the waves. On dry land, she's dragged down by the weight of so many things like the body she's never felt comfortable in. Here in the sea she can be herself, sleek and beautiful and unafraid.

The thought that something might be wrong with her sends panic clawing in my chest. This is my fault. I was the one who demanded to find the plant kids. Only thinking about myself, trying to prove I was good as people with powers.

Now we're no closer to finding Willow and Soo-yeon, all my friends are locked in cells, and my sister is very sick.

I hope nothing gets worse. "Does she have enough water?"

"I'm not sure. There's some in the cells, but you know what Airy's like."

We're close enough now that we can see my sister drifting among the cloud. It's something toxic leaking out of her pores. As we approach, her dark eyes flick open, swirling like there's poison trapped inside them.

"Hazy and Effie." She smiles, but I can see it takes effort. "You both came today."

"And what do I look like?" Hazel asks.

"A ferocious creature of tentacles and razor edges. A monster built for swallowing underwater kingdoms."

"The nightmare still holds then," she says sadly.

"I recognise Effie though." Airy's hair drifts all around her. "Eff, I'm so thirsty. I can feel myself drying out, like my cells are becoming dust inside me."

With an abrupt shift, all the water is gone. The three of us are crouched on the ground in the middle of an expanse of desert. The ground is dark brown and hard underneath us, cracks zig-zagging through it. Nothing grows here, and the only escape from the endless flat is the soaring shape of mountains in the distance, but they look as barren.

Airy flops on the ground, arching her back and gasping. "Water."

"We were just *in* the water," I squeak. "Hazel, takes us back there."

"It doesn't work like that." She shakes her head. "Dreams shift underneath you without warning. She's worried about drying out and so…"

"Think wet thoughts." I kneel beside Airy and stroke her forehead. It's dry and hot, almost burning the sensitive skin at my fingertips. "Close your eyes really hard and wish."

"Doesn't matter." She coughs dust. "Only a dream. More worried about dying in real life."

"You're not going to die." I squeeze her hand, but too hard, and I feel the skin split. Hot sand spills out, grains glowing white hot that burn my skin in individual pin-pricks. "We're going to save you."

"That's the spirit." She coughs weakly. "Little sib coming for me."

"I will." I kiss her forehead and my lips burn. "I promise I will."

"Please, Eff." Hazel clutches my hand. Squeezes it hard. I can feel the imaginary imprint of the gun against my fingers. "I can't do anything. You've got to save us."

I open my mouth to say something reassuring, but instead I'm looking at the ceiling of the little round room. The blankets are tossed all around me, as if I kicked them off when I was trying to swim in my sleep.

Cammie whimpers against me, twitching and mumbling.

I roll over, my eyes tracing the line of her cheek. I remember the way her and dream-Effie had been looking at each other.

She was dreaming of me.

It's not the time to be thinking of that. We need to mount a rescue before my sister dies.

"Cammie." I shake her shoulder. "You need to wake up. Now."

She makes a soft cry in her throat. "Monster."

"No. It's just a dream, and you're safe now. Well, safe enough."

One hand clutches my wrist and her eyes flutter open. "Safe?"

I smile down at her. "Yes, for now. Although I'm about to go and do something ridiculous."

She struggles into a sitting position. "I was dreaming. You were there and we were…" Her cheeks colour faintly. "It doesn't matter. The monster was there too, and we fled into the hedge maze but—"

"The monster is Hazel," I say. "She's trying to communicate with us through our dreams, but you've all been poisoned by nightmares."

"Oh!" She flushes darker. "That's embarrassing. I've been running away from her every night."

"You're not the only one, don't worry. But none of this matters, because my sister is dying, and we need to save her."

Cammie's eyelids flutter. "That'll be dangerous."

"Yes," I say simply.

"Together." She takes my hand and squeezes it hard. "We can do it together."

"Yes, we can. But we're going to need a plan."

NEITHER OF US have really made a plan before. Not for anything like this. We're hiding in a castle with mutants who will capture and zap us if they find us. The only advantage we really have is that Cammie knows the secret passages.

"Night's the best time," Cammie says. "They don't go to the cells at night. The wolves walk the halls, but they don't usually go all the way up the stairs. The problem is getting the cells open."

"We need to get all the keys, so we can get everyone out and plan a proper escape."

Cammie shakes her head. "They keep the keys in

the quarters where they stay. The only time they bring them out is to feed everyone, and the wolves and Flicker go then to make sure everyone behaves."

"Then we have to go into the quarters," I say firmly.

"They'll catch me, even if I'm invisible. There's always someone there."

"Not if I make a distraction."

Her eyes go even wider. "That's so dangerous! What are you going to do?"

I laugh. "I have no idea, but I'll figure something out. My sister's life is at stake."

Cammie touches me again, just a very gentle brush of her fingertips along the back of my hand. "You need to be *careful*, Effie. Don't let yourself get hurt."

"I'll be fine." My eyes catch hers and hold them. I have a crazy thought about what it would feel like to kiss her, which is the last possible thing I should be thinking about. I do wonder what she'd do. I'd have to ask permission first. Consent is important. But I need to rescue Airy first. Maybe if this all works out, and we're all still okay at the end, then I'll ask her.

The plan. Think about the plan, Effie.

I take a deep breath. "Okay, try this. You camouflage yourself at the entrance to the living quarters. I'll make an enormous commotion, hopefully enough to draw them all out. As soon as they're gone, you sneak in, get the keys and let the others out of the cells. Then you give me a signal and I'll find my way back here. Four-eighteen is the secret passage, right?"

"Yes." She beams at me. "The fourth column of bricks, eighteenth one down. That's the way off the staircase. And I know what we can do for a signal. There's a big gong in one of the chambers near the living quarters. Lupine uses it to summon the others. She always hits it three times, but I'll hit it once."

"Okay." Her hand is still on mine, but I hold out the other one to show how much it's shaking. "I don't know if I'm brave enough to do this, but I'm going to do it anyway."

"I think you're very brave," she whispers. "Doing this for your sister."

"I love her," I say simply. "Now let's go and do this."

We make our way out of the chamber and back down the secret passage that leads to the stairs. When we reach it, we both press our ears to the stone, but there's no sound from outside.

Cammie presses the indentation that opens the door. We both hold our breath as it grinds open. The stairs are completely silent. Moonlight spills through a window, painting them a faint grey. If they've been here hunting for me, they're elsewhere now.

"Good luck," I whisper. I can feel Cammie's hand on mine, even with her blended into the stone walls.

"You too." Her mouth is against my ear and I feel a brush of her lips as she moves them across my cheek. "I'll be ready for your distraction. You're very distracting, Effie." There's a very faint laugh as she lets go of my hand and is gone.

Which leaves me standing alone in the stairwell in the middle of the night, with no stealth powers, no defensive powers, and definitely no offensive powers.

There are wolves prowling the corridors, plus some girl who can zap people. Not to mention Lupine, who's scary enough on her own.

This is a terrible idea, but I need to do it anyway.

For Airy, and for my friends. For the kids we're supposed to be babysitting.

No time to waste. I take a deep breath, and begin to descend.

CHAPTER SEVENTEEN

IN WHICH I PRETEND TO BE A SUPERHERO, AND LEARN THAT IT'S HARDER THAN IT LOOKS ON TV

IT TURNS out it's super creepy sneaking through a giant old castle in the middle of the night, especially when you don't know what's around any corner. Somehow, I have to cause a commotion. The problem is I'm not really a commotion sort of person. I tend to follow the rules. I'm not sure if that comes from the Dark Year, where everything depended on appearing as quiet and normal as possible. If I didn't, my family would suffer, and I could never let that happen. Airy and my Dads depended on it, just like Airy and the plant kids need me right now.

I'll be whatever the plan needs me to be. That's how I'm going to save my sister.

I can be a silent ghost in the hallways, almost as invisible as Cammie.

I can be a rebellious monster, sowing chaos where I go.

At the bottom of the stairs, it's still silent. There are lit torches hanging on the walls, but most of them have been doused. A pair burns at each end, and in between is a long stretch of darkness. I peer into it, but see no sign of glowing wolf eyes.

I pause beside the last torch, at the edge of the darkness.

Hold on. Fire is a great opportunity to cause commotion. I reach up and tug at the nearest one. It's wedged in pretty good, but I finally manage to pull it out of its holder. It's heavier than I thought, and emits a thin black smoke. Still, now I have portable light and I also have a spark to start a bigger fire. The problem is the castle is made of stone and isn't going to burn easily. Although…

I make my way down the hallway as quickly as I can without making any noise. The torch is heavy in my hand, but I hold it high. At the end of the corridor it branches off to the left or right, or else you can go straight through the big double doors. I take a deep breath and hope that Lupine doesn't sleep on her throne, then turn around and push backwards through the doors.

The torch doesn't illuminate enough of the enormous room to see everything. In this space, it only casts a feeble pool of light. The moonlight makes the saints in the windows glow like they're faintly coloured ghosts. There's no sound aside from my own breath. Maybe wolves sleep really quietly, and they're curled up together, waiting for someone juicy to come along and present themselves as a snack.

"Effie knew this was a terrible idea," I whisper, but jump at the sound of my voice. Possibly better not to narrate this particular incident. I creep forward. The stone is very cold underfoot. I carry on until I can see the dim shape of the throne ahead. It's empty, and no beasts slumber at its base. I have a strange urge to sit, to see what it feels like to look down on the world, but instead I thrust the torch towards it.

I hold the flame right against the base of the seat. It does nothing. I stand there, feeling stupid, as the fire licks at the wood without really tasting it. Maybe it's treated with something that means it doesn't burn. There's other furniture piled up in the corners which might—

I stagger back as a burst of heat comes from the throne. The bottom is burning merrily now and the flames are eagerly scrambling to reach the back. Looks like I have a bright future as an arsonist if it comes down to it. It's no mutant power, but it'll do in a pinch. The flames make the whole room brighter, and I can see some of the broken furniture is wooden too. If I'm going to burn things down, I may as well do a thorough job of it. Most of the furniture is smashed up pews, and I feed a few more to the fire. It has enveloped the throne completely now and makes it look like the devil's favourite comfortable chair.

Now I have a massive fire burning in Lupine's throne room, but the problem is nobody's around to see it. Not such a great commotion after all. How do I get people in here without getting myself caught?

I inhale a bunch of smoke and start coughing. Oh yes. I forgot fires do a lot of that. I get to my hands and knees and start crawling out of the throne room.

It's getting uncomfortably hot in here, so I throw the torch into another pile of broken furniture and crawl faster.

The doors seem extra heavy when I pull them open. Over my shoulder, it's like a glimpse into hell, flames dancing and smoke billowing.

"Effie didn't know their own power." I break off coughing. "And was both surprised and terrified to find out how good they were at chaos."

I leave the door open to let smoke out into the castle where *eventually* someone has to realise. Maybe I should make some noise. Cammie's signal is a single bang on the gong, but if I just slam it a whole bunch of times it surely has to have a result.

Question is: where's the gong?

I head left first, and the corridor twists around until it comes out into a small room with a long table in it. There's still some plates sitting on it, although they've been cleaned of any food. It's a shame, because I'm starting to get hungry. At the far end of the room, I spot the giant round metal shape of the gong, hanging in an ornate wooden frame.

I also spot a wolf.

At first, I only see the glowing green eyes. Then it lifts one corner of its mouth in a snarl, and I see a flash of long, white teeth. It's a different kind of scared than when you get stopped at an army checkpoint. That's a cold fear that curls itself inside you and paralyses you with possibilities. You have to stop and carefully extract yourself from a situation like that. Be aware of your eyes and your hands and the way your weight shifts. All your words must be steady and respectful. Be anonymous.

When the wolf growls, it's a different kind of fear, one that plugs into a whole other part of my brain.

My knees tremble. My stomach feels loose and liquid. I can't think or plan a rational escape.

I turn and run.

The wolf howls. It's incredibly loud in the stone room. It echoes off the walls and gains strength, like a whole pack is calling down vengeance upon me. I go flying back down the corridor, past the smoke and heat pouring from the throne room and into the corridor that leads back to the stairs. No, I can't go this way. Cammie needs to come through here to set the others free.

There is something important and useful I can get my hands on though. I probably shouldn't have thrown my torch at the fire. Luckily there are more on the walls. This time I'm fuelled by panic and it's easier to pull on from the wall.

I run back past the throne room and head to the right. It's the opposite direction to where the wolf was.

When I glance over my shoulder, I see the pair of them, prowling towards me as if they have all the time in the world. They *know* they can beat me and drag me down. Or rather, Lupine knows, because she's in their minds like Wally said, watching me flee.

They growl, deep and ferocious. Their claws scrape against the stone. They're coming for me. It's not enough for the wolves alone to follow me. I need it to be Lupine and her annoying henches too. That's the only way Cammie can get the keys and free the others.

I skid past a suit of armour, and come to a halt. It's uncomfortable, but I squeeze in behind it.

The wolves pad around the corner, muzzles raised and sniffing. I brace myself against the wall and shove forward as hard as I can. The suit of armour tips and topples forward, crashing to the ground.

One of the armoured gauntlets hits a wolf across the nose and it yelps. I feel bad, because it's not their fault they've been hijacked by Lupine. The sound of it crashing to the ground gives both wolves pause. One has its head lowered, as if it wants to run, but Lupine's voice in its mind is keeping it in place.

I wave the torch in front of their faces and crouch to pick up the pointy metal thing the suit of armour was holding onto. I'm sure it has a name, but I don't know what it is. All I care about is that it could keep the wolves at bay.

Between the torch and the sharp point, they're hesitant. I back slowly away, but the wolves jostle for space as they match me pace for pace. Both are growling, a rumbling sound that travels through me. The torch shakes in my hand, but I hold it tight. It's the only thing stopping me from getting pounced on.

"I don't want to hurt your wolves," I shout. "But I will if I have to. Call them off."

Deep down, I'm not sure if I could bring myself to actually hurt the wolves. Even though my brain is terrified of them, I know they're scared of the fire and the blade too. If they throw themselves onto me, it will be Lupine doing it because she doesn't care about them.

I keep edging back down the corridor. With a glance over my shoulder, I can see there's a corner up ahead. I have no idea what's around it. Hopefully not a wider area where the wolves can do a pincer move against me. I need to make a stand somewhere.

Two more steps and I run up against a wall. One that shouldn't be there. I press my hand backwards, and it's too smooth to be stone. Which means...

"Yes, that's it," a woman's voice says. "You've got the little brat."

Following the wolves, three human figures come into view. Even though this is terrible, and I should be terrified, there's a wild, excited part of me that knows the plan is working. I've sowed chaos. I've caused a commotion. Now Cammie will be in their quarters, taking the keys.

Now all I need to do is stall them until I hear the gong.

I squeeze my weapon tighter in my hand. "Drop the forcefield, or the wolves die."

CHAPTER EIGHTEEN

IN WHICH I LEARN THAT SOMETIMES PEOPLE CAN SURPRISE YOU

"YOU WOULDN'T HURT THE WOLVES," Wally says. He's closer now, and I can see his sister behind him. She looks like a sharper, meaner version of her brother, with the same slim build and floppy hair. Her hand twitches restlessly at her side, like she constantly has electrical current running through it. Tiny sparks drip from her fingers and onto the floor.

"Stop talking, Wally," she says. "You're supposed to deal with the fire."

Lupine glides up to the forcefield, standing so close that the tip of her nose flattens against the surface. "Not yet. I have questions to be answered. Uppermost in my mind being how you got out of your cell."

"I may not be a mutant, but I have skills." I try to sneer, but I'm not very good at it.

"You expect me to believe you picked the lock on the cell?" The girl is much better at sneering than me. "I bet Wally let you out. He's got a crush on you."

"Shut up, I do *not*." His face is really red, so he's not

a very good liar. I don't have a crush back, because even if he has a nice face, he's working for the *bad guy*. And besides, when I think the word 'crush', another face pops into my head.

"Wally knows better than to let anyone go." Lupine's voice is so cold it makes me shiver.

I meet her gaze, and it takes every tiny piece of strength in me not to flinch away. "He didn't do anything. You learn a lot in the Dark Year." It's true. You learn to lie and to evade patrols, to pick locks and steal, to hide contraband in your shoes. To look invisible, a ghost of a kid treading very lightly on the world.

"Why didn't you rescue your friends if you're so good at lock picking?" Flicker asks stubbornly.

Oh, great. Thank you so much, you annoying girl. That's a very good question.

"They're not my friends." The lie tastes horrible in my mouth, because it skates too close to one of my biggest fears. But I use it because it's so close to believable. "I'm a baseline. Why would they care about me?"

I can see that they believe it, all three of them. It makes me feel even worse, like I've accidentally told the truth. But no. I'm doing this for my friends. We're a team. They'll be here for me when I need them. And right now, I'm buying time to save them.

There are still two big problems.

Number one, I still haven't heard the gong.

Number two, I'm stuck. Even if Cammie gets the others out, I'm still in a forcefield with Lupine glaring at me.

The forcefield opens for a brief moment, but only

long enough to let Flicker inside. She grins at me and takes a couple of quick steps forward.

I jab the metal stick in her direction. "Back off. I don't trust any of you. Wally's a liar and both of you just want to *hurt me*." I don't need to act for that last part.

"Fighting us will only make this worse," Flicker says. "You can't win. You don't even have any powers. You're just a b—"

I jab the end of the pole forward. She's too busy being sassy that she doesn't react in time, and it smacks her right in the mouth. Wally lets out a strangled gurgle of laughter.

"Enough," Lupine says. "Wally, shrink the forcefield tighter."

"No!" Flicker scrambles to her feet and lunges for me. I shove the pole at her again, but this time she catches it. It buzzes in my hand, and then something kicks me incredibly hard in the back. I tumble forward and land on my side, looking around wildly for my new attacker.

There's nobody there. It's an electric shock from Flicker, transmitted down the metal pole.

I feel the same kick again. My fingers are frozen tight to the weapon. I'm twitching all over and my jaw feels wired together. For a moment, the tight feeling ebbs and my body is filled with a million pins and needles, pressing from the inside against every part of my skin.

I moan through clenched teeth.

Flicker looks down at me with a smirk.

I manage to unhinge my jaw and scream, in the hope it will ease some of this impossible pain. My voice tears. It sounds electronic. And somewhere, underneath it all, I hear the echoing sound of the gong.

That single ringing note is almost enough to make up for how I'm feeling.

It says that my friends are going to be free. Airy's going to be safe, because there's no way Hazel will let her down.

Cammie will get out of there too.

Everyone's okay except for me, lying on the floor, twitching and screaming while three mutants look down at me. Lupine is bored, Wally looks like he's about to cry, and Flicker looks like a scientist taking notes.

"That's enough," Lupine says. "Give the baseline a moment to recover, and then take them up to the cells. Flicker, go with your brother and make sure this troublemaker is locked in *properly* this time. I'll take care of the fire."

She stalks off with the wolves, leaving me with the siblings. This actually scares me *more* than when Lupine is there to keep a leash on Flicker.

"Are you okay?" Wally crouches down beside me.

"Why do you care?" I croak.

"I don't know. It's not because of any crush. But, like, you don't seem like you belong here. Even if you did stand there with a pike and a torch, threatening Lupine's wolves." There's a tiny smile tucked in the corners of his mouth, like he's secretly impressed with me.

Not that it matters, since I'm at their mercy.

"Whatever. Just take me back to my cell," I mumble. It would be great if I could come up with some other amazing escape plan, but my body feels like it's on fire and my head is empty.

"Help me up with them, Flick."

"You going to behave? Or do I need to give you another buzz?" She flips her hair out of her face and grins down at me. She might be just as pretty as her brother, but her electric hands make me cringe away.

"Don't touch me." I push myself up and get gingerly to my feet. Everything still hurts.

Flicker shrugs and picks up the torch, and kicks the metal pole into the corner. "As long as you're nice and quiet, we don't have to do anything."

"You can't walk on your own after a zap like that," Wally says. "Believe me, I know."

I shuffle towards the wall and place one hand on it. "I'll be fine."

"Your crush is a stubborn one," Flicker says. "I like them."

"Will you *shut up*?" I'm too tired and sore to be polite anymore. I close my eyes as the world swims around me. "Your voice is worse than your electric touch."

Wally steps alongside me, holding onto my elbow. "Look, you might be as crazy as my sister in your own way, but we'll be here all day if you insist on getting to your cell under your own steam."

"Fine." I let myself collapse slightly onto him, just to ease the burden.

The next thing I know, he's carrying me, which is very annoying. It does make it a lot easier getting up the stairs though, because they're steep and cold. I'm shivering by the time we reach the top.

I'm so exhausted, I almost forget what we're going to find.

My friends didn't even bother to close the cell doors on their way out. I suppose they were in a big hurry. It makes things really bad for me, though. Maybe they'll hurt me for real this time. I cling to the small satisfaction that I got the others out. Me, no powers at all, fighting off these three mutants. Saving the day.

"What?" Flicker runs down the row of cells, banging door after door. "Where did they go?"

"This was you." Wally drops me on the floor and joins Flicker looking in the cells, even though it's obvious nobody's in them. He whirls to look at me. "How did you do this? You were lying about being a baseline, weren't you?"

It hurts to laugh, but I can't stop. "No." I waggle my hands. "I've got nothing."

"Then how did they get out of here?" Flicker strides back toward me. She bends down and puts one hand around my neck. "You better give me some answers or else."

I cough something between a laugh and a sob. "I'm the one person who wasn't here and the one person without powers. You locked up a bunch of mutants in ordinary cells and thought that was enough? Hazel probably dream-walked into your mind and read something out of it."

Flicker squeezes harder but there's no electricity coming from her fingers. "Dream-walked? She can do that?"

"Does it to my sister all the time. They've got superpowers, remember?"

She shoves me backwards so I sprawl on the ground. "Wally, put up a forcefield at maximum range. Surround the castle and the grounds. They've probably run, so let's make sure they don't get far. Then go find Lupine and let her know. I'll watch this one here. I still don't trust them."

Wally's mouth moves. He's probably looking for an excuse, but he thinks better of it and goes racing off down the stairs. Part of me hopes my friends got out before Wally got his forcefield up. The rest of me desperately wishes they stuck around for me. At least if they escaped, they can bring reinforcements. Ones like Biome, Ms. Sefo and Dragon. Real superheroes, not scrawny little human kids like me.

Flicker sits down cross-legged beside me. "I can't figure you out, Effie. That's your name, right? That's a human name, not a mutant name?"

"It stands for Finn Elizabeth." I don't know why I'm telling her this, but as long as we're talking, she isn't zapping me. "I get a typical boy's and girl's name to use if I want, but I chose Effie to stay neutral."

"I like that." She nods. "I sometimes think I might be sort of a boy, like deep down."

"Maybe you are. You're the one who'd know, but I get that it can be confusing."

"And your sister is the fish girl, right? Except she was born a boy."

"She was always a girl," I say. "It doesn't matter what she was born as. Her birth name was Amari Josiah, but her mutant name is Ariel."

Flicker laughs. "Like from *The Little Mermaid*?"

"Well, yeah. It was her favourite movie for way too long, even before she got powers."

"My name's Jolene, like the song. Pretty terrible, huh? I was so happy when I went through the change and could pick a new name."

I give her my most unimpressed look. "And you chose Flicker? That's so bad."

For some reason, she finds this hilarious and bursts out laughing. I stare at her while she carries on for a few seconds. Then she stops dead, like a switch has been flicked, and slowly slumps over onto her side.

"Bang." Deadshot steps out from the stairwell into the corridor. "Told you I was a dead shot." She winks at me. "Nice work on the rescue, Effie. Now it's our turn to return the favour. Let's get you out of here."

CHAPTER NINETEEN

AND NOW I NEED YET ANOTHER PLAN?
SERIOUSLY? THIS IS A NIGHTMARE!

"DEADSHOT!" I gape at her.

"Yes, I'm here to save the day. Don't look so surprised." Her strawberry blonde hair is tangled messily around her face and her lips are bruised, but it's still wonderful to see her. I never thought I would think that about Deadshot.

"You came to save *me*. That's what I'm surprised about."

"I owe you, apparently." She gives me the tiniest of smiles. "But if this is going to work, we need to get moving."

"Is everyone else okay?" I ask, still sitting on the ground.

"Yes, sorry. I should have led with that. Hazel's taken Airy off to the well for emergency water supply. The others are in the hidden passage."

"Okay." I struggle to my feet. "You might need to help me. I got a bit zapped. I'm sorry that you have to touch a baseline, but it's the only way."

"Effie," Deadshot says, but then doesn't follow it up with any other words. Instead, she crosses over to me, and slips her arm through mine. Then we limp to the door to the stairs.

"Sorry." It's very difficult going down, given that my legs still aren't working well and my head aches every time we thump down a step. "I'm slow and useless, but you already know that, don't you?"

Deadshot makes a little frustrated sound in her throat, which I assume is at me, for being the most pathetic baseline she ever had the misfortune to meet, but she doesn't let go of my arm and keeps guiding me down the stairs. "I've got a pocket full of stones, and I'll use them on whatever and whoever I have to."

"Don't hurt the wolves," I say.

"Fine. I'll only throw the stones at people who deserve it."

"Fair." I clench my fist at my side. "Now let's go find Willow and Soo-yeon."

Deadshot shakes her head. "They're somewhere out into the grounds where the wolves are patrolling and who knows what else now."

I frown and wish I was strong enough to go running down the stairs and away. "Didn't think you'd be scared, Deadshot."

"I'm being smart. We need to find the others. If I let you run off to find the kids when you're shakier than a newborn lamb… let's say a lot of people are going to be mad at me, and I don't need that."

"Fine." My legs *are* very wobbly. I hope the tree-house Hazel saw in the plant kids' dreams is real. What if they're scared and alone, going through their own Dark Year? We have to rescue them, and *soon*.

We finally reach the entrance to the passageway, and I count out the bricks.

"There." I gesture like a magician as the dark entrance is revealed. "I'm doing what I'm told."

I shuffle into the cramped passageway and push the button to close it. As soon as it closes behind us, I'm hit with a huge wave of dizziness. Being in the darkness makes it impossible to see which way is up and I feel like I'm floating in space.

"I need to sit down," I say faintly.

"Not much room for sitting, but let's try." We both ease down the wall, until we're both wedged there. "Is that any better or worse?"

"Better. Not spinning in the dark so much."

"Good," Deadshot says, and an almost companionable silence falls.

Unfortunately, she won't let it last.

"Effie?"

"Yeah?"

"I want to apologise to you."

I have no idea what to say in response, but she rushes on ahead regardless.

"I guess it's obvious what for, but I was awful to you. It's not even really because of the human thing, although I suppose that was a little part of it."

"This isn't the best apology I've ever heard," I say dryly.

"Can you let me finish please, Effie?" Are those tears in her voice? "I'm so jealous of you. You have this perfect family and these awesome friends, while I'm stuck with Mrs. Harper in the home. It's so ungrateful to complain because at least I'm safe, but you have this perfect life on Mutopia, and I'm looking in from the outside while—" She breaks off. "You're right, this is a terrible apology. I was a loser and I was wrong."

"Yeah," I say. "You were. But like, you can still be friends with us, especially if you can stop being rude for a few seconds at a time."

There's a faint laugh from beside me. "Kel hates me though."

"Oh." For some reason, I can't stop smiling, even though it's super obvious and also slightly irritating. I can't help but feel warm fuzzy feelings towards this apologetic Deadshot who helps me down the stairs and confesses things to me in the dark. "You like Kel."

"I don't *like* her. Maybe she's pretty and funny, but she's still the most annoying person I've ever met."

"You like her so much." I can't stop laughing.

"She hates me though."

I think about Kel telling me that I could hit her with a rock if she ever liked Deadshot. It was pretty unconvincing. Then there was the archery dream. I don't even know whose it was.

"I don't think Kel hates you."

"She'd never *like* me though."

"That's where having a fraction more chill might help you." I put my hand on hers and squeeze it. "I'll also make sure she knows what an amazing rescue you did. Saving her friend has got to score you points, right?"

"Thanks," she whispers, and rests her head on my shoulder which takes me by surprise so much I almost jump out of my skin. It's actually kind of nice, even though it's Deadshot.

"I think I'm feeling better now," I say. "I'm probably up to crawling down to the others. I've just got one more question."

"Okay?" She sounds nervous.

"Why did you decide to apologise now?"

"First I woke up in a cell, and my first thought was whether you and Kel and the others were okay. That was my first clue that maybe I'd caught feelings somewhere along the way. Then you were brave enough to stand up to these mutants on your own, and I realised that I'd been the worst of the worst. I was scared to do it and I've *got* mutant powers."

"You still came and saved me," I say. "And I think Kel likes things that are the worst, so you've got that going for you."

"Wow, maybe I do still hate you."

"I hate you too." I squeeze her hand one last time and begin to shuffle down the passageway. When I finally see the light, I get tears in my eyes, and by the time I tumble down the hole and collapse on the floor, I'm actually crying.

"You're okay!" Cammie is teary-eyed too, kneeling beside me and touching my face. "I was so worried."

"We all were," Dopple says. "Deadshot went off to rescue you and it took *ages*."

Kel punches me in the shoulder, and then hugs me so tight I gasp. "I was mad. What do you call running off on your own and confronting mutants and wolves and whatever else?"

"Bravery." I pull back so I can smile at her, but she grabs me tighter and shoves her face into my shirt.

"Yeah? Well, don't you make a habit of it. It's bad for my health, worrying about you so much."

"No faith in me. Plain old hero, none of the super."

We finally manage to part. Kel's eyes are serious for, like, the second time I've ever seen in my life. "So there's some good news, but we're still kinda screwed though, right?"

I can't really deny it, but I find my mouth gabbling anyway. "Start with the bad news. Airy and Hazel are in a well, and the rest of us are hiding in the walls. There's a forcefield around the castle stopping us from leaving, and we still have no idea where the plant kids are."

"That's about it," Dopple says gloomily. "The only thing we've got going for us is that we're not locked up anymore."

"Which is a lot," Deadshot says with surprising loyalty. "Thanks to Cammie and Effie."

"Did someone hit you on the head?" Kel asks her.

"Be nice," I say sternly.

"To Shottie? Really? Did someone hit *you* on the head?"

"Hush." I laugh, but it hurts. "We're going to have to work together to get this done. The first priority is taking out Wally, the forcefield boy. That means we can get out, and more importantly, we can let other people *in*."

"The wolves are a problem," Cammie says. "They're prowling everywhere, and they're not the only animals under her control. It's like an evil version of Snow White cleaning the house."

"I don't want to hurt the animals," Dopple says.

"Nor does Princess-slash-Prince Effie here." Deadshot ruffles my hair. "So let's try taking out Wolf Lady, and see if that frees the poor pups."

"Don't forget Flicker." I shudder. "She's dangerous." Even though our last conversation was actually relatively normal, a few minutes earlier she'd had her hand around my throat. I don't think she'd hesitate to do it again, given the chance.

"She might not be a problem," Deadshot says. "I nailed her pretty hard in the temple."

"The problem is we don't have a lot of firepower," Kel says. "If I get a run-up, I can do a lot of damage, but all these narrow corridors are really bad for acceleration. Which leaves us with dear Shottie again, throwing bullets."

"We're talking about really hurting people." Dopple's voice is really quiet and he won't look at any of us. "Maybe worse than that. Because if we don't, the forcefield goes back up, or the animals attack, or Flicker gets her hands on us."

"You're saying I have to kill them." Deadshot's voice seems to bounce off the walls.

"No," I say. "There's got to be a better way. We need a smarter plan. Stop Wolf Lady, save the kids, get out of here."

Everyone goes quiet after that. They're all looking

at me. Probably because I half-shouted at them and implied there was a smarter plan. So it's up to me to come with that plan. Except really I've got nothing.

"Wally has a crush on me," I say. "Maybe I can use that."

"Wait," Cammie says, looking at me with narrowed eyes. "What?"

"Maybe I can distract him with my, uh, my wiles? Is that what you call those? And then someone can knock him out and Kel can run for help."

"Do you have wiles?" Kel asks me. "I've seen no evidence."

I glance at Cammie, who's blatantly saying nothing, so maybe I was completely wrong about that. I have no idea how to flirt anyway, so I'm not sure what I'd say to convince Wally to come off into a dark corner with me so someone can tie him up.

"Fine." I scowl. "That was a bad idea. So here's another one. We get Hazel out of the well and get her to shoot them with Nightmare. Then we walk through their dreams and make them scared of each other. Divide and conquer."

"Risky," Dopple says. "We have no idea if that's even possible."

"It's worth a try, isn't it?" Cammie asks. "Worst case scenario, it fails and we've got a bunch of jumpy villains for Deadshot to throw stones at. In the meantime, I'll find a way to the tower." She smiles at me, with enough warmth that it makes me think I might have wiles after all. "It's a great idea, Effie."

"Even I like it," Deadshot says. "Which means it must be good."

Kel snorts. "If I was the naturally suspicious type, I'd think you're working for the villains, and trying to betray us."

"I'm not." Deadshot's eyes go wide and she looks at me imploringly. "Tell her, Effie."

"Shottie's a changed girl," I say. "And she's going with you, Kel, when you go to fish Hazel out of the well."

"I still don't like that name," Deadshot says with an eye roll, but she mouths 'thank you' at me from behind Kel's head. Oh my god, does she think this is a date? This is not remotely a date. *Or* an opportunity for her to flirt with one of my best friends.

"The important thing is getting Hazel and bringing her back here," I say.

"Yes, yes, we know." Kel grins at me. "I think I like this bossy, know-it-all Effie."

"I'm trying to save us all!" I protest. "I'm not being *bossy*."

Kel and Cammie both snort, which seems entirely unfair.

"Better do what the boss orders," Kel says. "We'll fetch Hazel and then..." Her grin gets wider. "We unleash nightmares."

CHAPTER TWENTY

YES, A LITERAL NIGHTMARE

IT'S VERY NERVE-WRACKING, being stuck in a secret chamber while two of your friends go sneaking off through certain danger. It's also strange thinking of Deadshot as a friend, rather than an angry girl who's waiting for a chance to punch me in the face. I remember how she laid her head on my shoulder in the darkness. Do people really change that much? Which part of her was an act? Maybe she really *is* betraying us, and leading Kel into another trap right now.

"Scared?" Cammie asks me. Her eyes are gentle, and her voice is soft.

I nod.

"Me too. I've been scared this whole time." She wriggles a little closer to me. "I was least scared last night."

"Oh." I blink at her. Does she mean when we were curled up together in the blankets? She's sitting very close to me now, her shoulder pressed against mine. My hand is resting on the ground and hers drifts down so it's sitting on the floor. There's a fraction of an inch separating us from touching. It's silly to be concerned about this, because we were pressed right up against each other in the tunnel and her lips were actually on my cheek when she wished me good luck. Yet here I am, obsessed with the tiniest distance.

Dopple sits on my other side, humming annoyingly loudly and inspecting his fingernails. Yes, Dopple, they are too long and need a cut. Is there a mood for him to ruin, or am I reading it wrong?

My finger twitches, bridging that tiny fraction. It touches Cammie's. I hear her inhale. She felt it too. Her weight shifts, leaning against me more. Then her hand moves too, sliding under mine like it's finding safety there. Her head tilts too, resting on my shoulder, and I don't know what chemistry is involved, but it's one hundred percent different than when Deadshot did it. I feel like I'm in the middle of sprinting for my life, but I also want to sing or do *something* to let the world know this is happening.

We sit like that for ages. I don't even pay attention to the passage of time. I'm aware Deadshot and Kel are out there, but I'm sitting in the middle of a magic spell made of bodies and contact and heartbeats.

"Less scared now?" Cammie whispers, at some point.

"Yes," I whisper back and curl my fingertips around her open palm.

"No," Dopple says. "I'm still terrified. Where *are* they?"

Kel pokes her head down from the ceiling, as if

she's been waiting for someone to ask just so she can have a dramatic reveal.

"Honestly, Dopple, you are so impatient. We've just been risking our lives while you're sitting pretty, or at least kinda cute, on your—" She breaks off and looks at me with narrowed eyes. "What is this thing?"

"What thing?" I blink up at her.

"It's about time." She beams at Cammie. "Nice work, chameleon girl."

"What are you talking about?" I ask, but Kel lets out a squawk because someone has shoved her through the ceiling from behind. I assume it's Deadshot, but Hazel's head appears next.

"Effie, thank goodness. I told Airy you were fine, but she's been worried."

"Is she here?" My heart is thumping again.

"No, I left her in the water. She's still recovering. She's fine though, I promise." She drops down and lands lightly on the ground. "I hear this dream-crashing thing is all your plan."

"Not really a plan." My voice squeaks. "Just an idea."

"A good one." Hazel flexes her hand, and Nightmare appears, wreathed in smoke. The barrel sings softly, something deep and wordless. "Dreams are powerful. Especially since we'll be walking through them."

"You already shot them?" I ask.

"We got lucky," Deadshot says. "They were having a big argument at the entrance to the castle and Hazel shot them all at once. Blam-blam-blam." She mimes the shooting of a gun.

"So what next?" I ask.

"They sleep." Hazel raises her eyebrows. "Perchance to dream. Where they'll find me." She smiles, and I can see a ghost of the nightmares in her expression—her teeth extended to fangs, something white and milky floating behind her eyes. It fades quickly, although I can't stop myself shivering slightly. "And you, Effie. You're good at navigating dreams, it turns out, plus you've talked to them most and know their weaknesses."

"Didn't she interrogate all of you?" I ask.

"Mostly about Mutopia," Dopple says. "Lots of questions about how it works."

"Lots about Biome too," Kel says. "Our wolf lady is pretty fixated on them."

"She's planning an attack, I'm pretty sure." Hazel frowns. "Presumably using Willow and Soo-yeon as hostages to provide some leverage, although it seems like it'll backfire. I can't imagine Dani and Dylan taking that well, and the others worship the ground those kids grow in." The corner of her mouth lifts. "You don't want to see the Cute Mutants angry."

"So the plan is to sleep?" Deadshot asks. "That seems, like, a massive letdown or something."

"Dreams are powerful," Hazel says. "More than most people know. You can sow ideas in them that burst forth much later as fruit. For example, perhaps the people you hate might not be so scary after all, and the fears might be in your own heart."

Deadshot turns to stare at her. "Wait... you mean?"

Hazel grins. "It only works if the ideas land in

fertile soil. It's more a gentle nudge than anything more sinister. There are ideas and beliefs people have deep down in the muck, too buried for them to see clearly. Dreams and nightmares can bubble them up to the surface."

"She's saying you thought we were secretly cool all along." Kel bats her eyelashes.

Deadshot splutters, but she doesn't deny any of it. I wonder if Hazel saw Kel in Deadshot's dream, or if that's a newer development. I can't *believe* I'm actually shipping them now. Is Kaleidoshot a good ship name?

"Count me in," Dopple says. "Finally an idea that doesn't sound deadly."

"A little scarier for those of us who travel." Hazel looks at me, her expression serious. "Nightmares can be terrifying, Effie."

"I've been scared before." My voice wobbles. "I'll survive."

"Good kid." She winks at me. "I'll see you in my dreams."

IT TAKES me a long time to fall asleep, even though I'm exhausted. Events have been so hectic and over-whelming that my body keeps twitching awake, worrying about where the next danger is coming from.

"Relax, Eff," Hazel says from somewhere nearby in the darkness. "Stop thrashing about."

I close my eyes and concentrate on my breathing,

trying to tune out the noise of other people breathing or lightly snoring. It's an effort to force thoughts of Airy out of my head, but I do it. This is how we make it safe for her. All I need to do is…

I open my eyes, and I'm in a forest. The trees are tall and thick, rising high above. Sunlight drifts through the leaves above, casting patterns on the ground. It reminds me of the Crown back on Mutopia. I wonder if Cybele is here, moving like a breeze through the trees. I wonder if she regrets not giving me powers now that I really need them. Maybe something super powerful like telekinesis or being able to shoot lasers from my eyes.

"There you are."

I turn to see Hazel, dressed in jeans and a t-shirt that says *Monster Girl*. Her hair glows in the warm light, like it's refracted into a thousand rainbows. "Whose dream is this?"

"Mine." She looks up at the forest canopy above. "This is one of my happy places. Whenever I'm stressed or worried, I come here. Sometimes the plant kids or Biome are with me, but they're always blooming quietly."

"I came here once," I tell her. "Except it was the middle of the night."

"You're not supposed to go in the forest." She wags her finger at me, mock-stern. "I thought everyone knew that."

"It was to beg a favour from Cybele." I'm not sure where to look. "I wanted powers."

"That makes sense. Must be tough, living on Mutopia without them. I used to be *so jealous* of Dylan, you have no idea. Here's my step-sib, who's already funny and clever, and they get superpowers, awesome friends, and the most badass girlfriend. And there I was, just a boring girl going to school and living the most boring life."

"I think I have some idea," I say quietly.

"Maybe so." She reaches out and nudges my shoulder. "Anyway, I was lucky enough to get them in the big awakening after Cybele woke up properly again. It felt like a dream come true, but they do come with a price. Sleep has never been the same since, and you have to choose when to use them. It's easier said than done. I probably shouldn't have shot Deadshot and Firewing for the bullying thing. The nightmares can last a while."

"You won't get any arguments from me." I glance at her. "Sometimes people need to be taught a lesson."

"It's done, anyway. With Wolf Lady, the decision's easy. She deserves a nightmare for sure. It's hard to get a read on the other two. Pretty sure Flicker gets too much pleasure from using her power, but the other kid seems more conflicted."

"Like you say, it's done." I grit my teeth. "So let's visit a nightmare."

"Sure." She hooks her thumbs in her belt. "Let's get a few things out of the way up front. Nightmares are scary, even other people's. However these guns work, they definitely feed on some creepy stuff in people's heads. Sometimes it's even worse than your own nightmares, to see what haunts others." She flexes her right hand and Dream appears in it. In one swift motion, she lifts it and presses it against the side of my head.

I try not to flinch. "Um, Hazel?"

"Listen to her song. The way that melody rises? Remember that."

It's true. Coming from the barrel of the gun is a thin, twisting song that rises up and then bursts like fireworks. It's naggingly infectious.

"So the rules. Stick with me. Don't believe anything you see. Do exactly what I tell you. And if for some reason, it all goes wrong, remember this tune and sing it as loud as you can. Dream will come and lead you to me."

"If it all goes wrong?" I clutch onto her arm.

"This is where sticking with me and doing what you're told is important. If you do that, everything will be fine. It depends how much like your sister you are. Airy has a knack for trouble, and is far too prone to going off and investigating bizarre nightmare occurrences."

"That does sound like her. I'm the sensible one though, haven't you figured that out yet?"

"Airy says that too." Hazel looks at me, face half bathed in sunlight. "She says it's because of the Dark Year. I spent it all asleep in an asteroid, so I missed the whole thing, but it sounds like it was tough for you."

I shake my head. "It was easy. All I had to do was stay quiet and keep my mouth shut."

Hazel makes a noise somewhere between sympathy and frustration. "Okay, well you can talk to me, unless I say to be quiet."

"And then I listen and do what I'm told." I grip her arm tighter. "I'm not Airy, don't worry."

"Okay, get ready." She holsters Dream, and Nightmare appears in her hand instead. "Let's get dark and freaky."

Hazel pulls the trigger.

The forest becomes shreds of darkness, as if it's been torn apart by the wings of a million birds.

I scream. Hazel smiles.

We fall into the storm.

CHAPTER TWENTY-ONE

IN WHICH I LEARN THAT THE INSIDES OF MINDS ARE SCARY PLACES TO SPEND TIME IN

FALLING through the nightmare is like diving into a pitch-black tunnel with a gale raging inside it. My breath is caught in my throat and I can't scream again. In Hazel's hand, Nightmare looks like a cannon. I can see all the detail on the barrel, the ornate carvings of interleaved skulls and crows and occult symbols. The word Nightmare glows a furious silver, as if the moon is melting inside the barrel and it's bleeding out. It howls, a ferocious mirror of the joyful melody that Dream sings.

Hazel is grinning, except it's not her usual smile. It's the smile of something that looks on all the things that humans and mutants do, and laughs at the futility and pettiness. A monster from outside that wants to snuff out the warmth of the fires that hold off the night. Her eyes are holes of darkness with cold blue lights emanating from deep inside. The flickering wings around us give off a reddish glow which highlights her elongated teeth.

I feel my grip on her loosen. Surely this cannot be—

"Hold on tight, Effie, for goodness' sake." Her voice is the same as ever. "It's just the border. If we had a mirror, you'd see you look just as frightful as me, you little monster. Close your eyes if you have to, because if you let go, you might end up with something that only looks like me. Something much hungrier."

Her voice splinters into static, but I squeeze my eyes closed and cling tight. My heart beats so fast, it might explode out of my chest. If you die in a dream, do you die in real life? I don't want to ask Hazel right now but—

The howling sounds die away abruptly. There's no more sensation of falling, and I can feel ground underfoot.

"Are we safe?" I whisper.

"Not sure about safe, but we're *here*," Hazel says.

I peek one eye open, and I'm standing outside the castle, although it's been scribbled over so the outlines of it are jagged. The sky overhead is a malevolent red. Something makes a croaking sound, and it's joined by a chorus of others. There's a flickering on the castle, and I realise it's covered by thousands of birds.

There's a ragged scream, except it's not my voice. There's a girl standing near us with floppy brown hair and a sneer. Flicker. Her hand twitches and sparks.

At the sound, all the birds launch themselves from the castle at once. They spread their wings wide and coast on the warm, damp breeze. Their eyes are a virulent, hypnotic green, just like the wolves. Like Lupine.

"She always watches you." Hazel's whisper is sibilant like a snake's. "Lupine knows every move you make. All your feeble plans are nothing but cold grey ash."

Flicker doesn't seem aware of us, like we're a lurking presence in her mind.

"No." Flicker's breath is rapid and squeaky. "We've been so careful."

The green lights above are as numerous as the stars on a pitch-dark night. Thousands of Lupine's eyes, transfixing Flicker with their gaze.

A rumbling sound comes from the castle, then four huge green orbs loom out of the darkness. They look like ghostly lights, come to haunt on the darkest night of the year. They draw closer, and steam pours from two huge, shaggy noses. Two wolfish mouths open, revealing huge slabs of tongue and glowing red throats. The teeth look like sharp blades of bone.

"We've been so hungry, little girl," one snarls.

"Lupine promised us a feast when this is done, yet we do not wish to wait," the other says.

"While she slumbers, we walk. Her clever monkey's brain is quiet, and we slip the leash."

"Now we snap up your few bites of flesh, crack your bones and drink the marrow."

"Hazel," I whisper.

She presses a finger to her lips. "Just stand back and let it happen naturally."

The wolves prow forward. Flicker turns to run, but she's too painfully, terribly slow. Enormous paws move across the ground, swallowing the distance between them like the tiniest bite. Their jaws unhinge enormously, like they want to devour far more than the fleeing figure of one girl.

I close my eyes. I can't watch this.

Flicker screams, a single high note that's cut off by the sound of crunching.

"And we didn't even need to do a single thing," Hazel says, sounding far too satisfied. "Sometimes their brains do it to themselves."

"You just watched her get eaten," I squeak, my eyes still firmly closed.

"It's only a dream, Eff. None of it's real. Flicker will wake uneasy with a sense she can't trust Lupine. This is the plan, remember? Besides, I've seen a lot worse things than that. The bonus of my mutant power. Now hold tight. We're in blank space, and we'll be shifting again."

I open my eyes briefly. Everything around me is grey and empty, filled with a drifting fog. It's slightly cool and I take a deep breath, just in time for us to be drowned out by the flickering of thousands of wings.

This time, I hold tight to Hazel. It's better to keep my eyes closed and ignore the wind rushing past. At least the journey is shorter this time. I stumble as we hit the ground.

Hazel squeezes my hand. "You can open your eyes."

We're standing in a small stone room with two beds in it. Aside from the extra sleeping space and more blankets on the beds, it's the same as the cell I woke up in. There's the same high window, not letting in enough light.

Lying on the bed, curled up and facing away, is

someone that looks like Flicker. The blanket is pulled up to bare shoulders and her hair is splayed out in the pillow.

"Do it," a voice says. "She has disobeyed too many times, and unlike you, she has not begged for forgiveness."

"I can't." My voice comes out as a croak. It's not my voice, it's Wally. In this dream we're inside his head. At his mercy. I start to panic, then I hear someone humming the infectious rise of the Dream melody.

It's Hazel, in here with me too. Letting me know this is okay.

"You must." Lupine's voice cracks in Wally's head like a whip.

"She's my sister. I love her."

"A flawed tool must be cast aside. Are you a broken thing too, Wally?"

The body we're trapped in moves. It feels clumsy, like a broken ride in an amusement park. Wally lurches upright and sways. He stumbles forward crookedly, like his legs are the wrong size. There's a mirror on the wall, and Wally stops to look at it. He splays his fingers on each side of the clouded glass and we all gaze upon his reflection. All the pretty autumnal joy of him is faded and battered, as if he's been drowned for too long in winter. The thing that truly startles me is the flicker of green in his eyes. It's the same as from Flicker's dream, in the eyes of the wolves and the crows. The sign of Lupine.

Fear curdles in my stomach.

Wally's dreaming of being controlled by Lupine, just

like one of her animals. Is this really something she can do? This is more terrifying than I imagined. His body moves over to the bed, staring down at his sister. Flicker twitches in her sleep. Her hair has tumbled down over her eyes. He moves to smooth it away, but his hand stops inches away.

"You only make this harder than it needs to be," Lupine's voice says in Wally's head. "Get it over with quickly, and we can move on with the plan."

"I can't do it without her." His voice is so broken it makes me want to cry.

"Then I shall turn your body around and march it out of here and throw it down the well, where you will drown in darkness."

I feel tears streaming down Wally's face as he takes the pillow from his bed and presses it with shaking hands over his sister's face. She wakes immediately, and thrashes underneath him. Her left hand jets out sparks.

"Ignore her," Lupine says. "Press harder."

I'm struggling to breathe. It's like I'm trapped in her head as well. I can't sense Hazel beside me. What if she's gone, and I'm left here to witness all—

Everything disappears, like a magician snapped their fingers, taking us back to the swirling grey fog.

"He woke up?" I ask. I'm shivering and there are tears on my face.

"No." I can't see Hazel, but her voice is gentle. "We didn't need to see any more of that."

"Nightmares." My teeth chatter. "They really are."

"My power." Hazel looms out of the mist, like an

ancient statue revealed. "It's sometimes a burden, Eff. What I find interesting is that we didn't really need to intervene. Both Wally and Flicker have nightmares that are already focused on Lupine."

"What does that mean?"

I can't see any horrors in Hazel's face. It's just my sister's best friend, looking a little bit scared. "It means the dominos are ready to fall. We only need the slightest push to send them crashing down." She draws Dream. Its barrel glows like the sunrise, shot through with pink and gold. The song that emanates from it pushes the fog away and brightens the expression on Hazel's face. "Take a good listen, because we've got one more nightmare to visit."

"Lupine." I'm even more scared of her now, after these nightmares we've watched.

"Remember those are their nightmares," Hazel says. "It's their brains dredging up their worst fears and presenting them. Doesn't make any of it real."

"I still hate her. I hated her before this."

"And how did you feel about Flicker?" Hazel asks.

I think about the fear in her eyes running from the wolves, and the way she looked, peacefully asleep as Wally approached her with Lupine inside his mind. "Her name's Jolene. And I feel sorry for her, but she's still dangerous. And Lupine is even worse."

"True." Dream disappears in Hazel's hand, and Nightmare glows there again, glittering like poisonous frost. "Let's see what the bully's afraid of, shall we?"

I close my eyes again as we fall through the darkness. This time it's far longer, and I start to worry that we're dropping down an endless hole. Hazel sings the melody from Dream, and I press my face against her shoulder, because I'm worried about what I'll see if I open my eyes.

When we finally land, I hear the sound of birdsong, and the wind in the trees. The breeze is cool, and smells of pine.

My eyes snap open.

CHAPTER TWENTY-TWO

YOU MIGHT NEED TO PEEK THROUGH YOUR FINGERS FOR THIS PART

WE'RE STANDING in a forest a lot like the one from Hazel's dream, except even more beautiful. The sound of running water comes from nearby. Brightly coloured birds flit from branch to branch. Huge boulders sit on the ground, covered in moss. They're in the vague shape of buildings, like something stood here once, and has been torn down by nature and time. I cross to one and try to run my fingers across it, to feel the age and weight, but my hand passes through it. I'm a ghost here. Hazel shakes her head and holds out her hand.

She's right. No matter how beautiful this is, it's still a nightmare.

Lupine bursts through the trees with a cracking and rustling. Her dress is torn and muddy, and she looks around herself, as if she's fleeing some unseen assailant.

"What have you done?" Her voice is high and wild.

"We've torn down your castle." Chatterbox steps

out from among the trees. Their eyes are the rich brown of freshly turned soil and their skin is a near-luminous green. The lotus flower at the hollow of their throat glows pink, and something writhes in its center. "And now is the moment of your end."

"My castle?" Lupine howls. "How? It's only been minutes."

"Nature will have her way." Chatterbox's teeth are a series of sharp and curving thorns. Their tongue is a tangle of vines braided together, and flickers like a snake's. "All the forest speaks to us, and we speak in return. The woman at the center of the world is our mother, and we are her furious will."

Marvellous drifts out from among the trees. Her feet don't even touch the ground. She's wreathed in leaves, and her eyes glow like twin hazel suns. "You stole our children." She thrusts her hands out, and vines erupt from the fingertips. They entwine Lupine all around until she's wrapped from head to toe, with gaps only for her eyes and mouth.

"I'm sure you had some *plan*." Chatterbox prowls across the ground. Venom glistens on the point of each tooth. "Some wicked design to bring us to heel."

"All I wanted—" Lupine begins, but her voice is cut off. She coughs and retches. Petals fall from her mouth in a torrent of purple and white and red. Vines spread her lips wide and the head of a vermillion rose pushes its way up out of her throat, spreading its petals and forcing her mouth into a painful oval.

Marvellous tilts her head. "You forfeited your rights the instant you laid your hands on our children."

"Nature is cruel." Chatterbox's grin stretches unnaturally wide. "And we are far, far crueler." They lunge forward, and their thorny teeth close tight around Lupine's throat. Blood sprays over their green skin. Their eyes twitch and burst, flowers springing from the sockets, and drinking into the blood, their pale pink petals turning wet and red.

Hazel leans forward and whispers in Lupine's ear. "The children did this. Flicker and Wally. They dropped the barrier and called Biome to you. They can't be trusted."

Chatterbox growls deep in their throat, a horrifying sound. My voice squeaks as I try to sing the melody from Dream's barrel, but the last two notes don't come out right.

"Oops, sorry." Hazel reaches up and covers my eyes. "Let's get out of here, Effie."

We tumble backwards, but when Hazel takes her hand from my face, we're back in the mist.

"That," I say, but further words are stuck in my throat.

"I should've made you close your eyes earlier. I didn't realise it would get so gruesome."

"That's not really them, is it?" My voice sounds like someone younger and more scared is talking. "Biome, I mean."

"It's a version of them constructed in Lupine's mind. Built from her fear of them."

"Because they wouldn't do something like that."

Hazel doesn't reply, and her expression is ghostly in the mist. "Let's get back. Based on these dreams, I think we're primed for fireworks. This plan of yours might work after all." She ruffles my hair, and draws Dream. It glows like the sunrise in her hands.

I WAKE up happy and relaxed. I'm not sure *exactly* what I was dreaming about, but my body feels loose and boneless. I'm lying in between Hazel and Cammie, and I look up at the ceiling with a smile spreading across my face.

"You're welcome." Hazel laughs. "I thought you could do with a nice dream send-off after all those horrors."

I sit bolt upright as memories crash back into my head. Flicker running from the wolves. Wally with a pillow in his hands. Lupine helpless at the hands of Biome. All these nightmares, running through their mind, spat from the guns that Hazel holds so gently.

"Did it work?" Dopple sits against the wall, yawning.

"We think so." Hazel gets to her feet and stretches. "And we didn't even have to do much. Once they wake up, we should start seeing fireworks."

"Do you think they'll run?" I ask. "Flicker and Wally, I mean."

Hazel shrugs. "Can't predict it for sure, but that's Plan A. If those two bail and bring the barrier down with them, it leaves only Lupine for us to deal with, and we can deal with her while Kel gets back with reinforcements."

"So while Lupine and the wolves are distracted, I'll find Willow and Soo-yeon," Cammie says.

"I'll come with you." I'm not sure whether it's the aftereffects of the good dream I was left with, or seeing the cracks of tension spreading between our captors, but I want to help *more*.

"I can sneak more easily on my own." Her eyes meet mine. "I mean, normally I'd love for you to come with me, but—"

"Finding the kids is the most important," Hazel says. "And more eyes is better. We want to make sure Lupine can't use the kids as hostages when we make our move."

"Good." I get to my feet. "Then stop wasting time and let's go."

"What did you see in those nightmares?" Cammie asks with this little smile. "You're all, like..."

"Like a superhero." There's no smirk on Deadshot's face for once. "We're going to do this together, right? Like the Cute Mutants."

"Can you all stop talking?" Kel groans, still tangled among the blankets.

Deadshot nudges her with one foot. "We're assembling, you annoying girl. You're supposed to be faster than any of us."

"You should have told me we were doing something *interesting* instead of just talking about it." Kel bounds to her feet, rainbow light dazzling all of us. "If we're gonna fight, I'm your number one girl."

Deadshot practically has heart eyes looking at her, and I half-expect her to make some proclamation of love like *you sure are my number one girl* and I start giggling.

Everyone stares at me.

"It's fine," I splutter. "I'm fine. Nothing's funny. Let's go fight some bad guys."

We haul through the hole in the roof and inch through the tiny narrow passageway in single file. Everyone's excited about the plan working. Maybe Hazel shot us all with Dream and infected us with positivity. I feel half-certain we'll get out and find the castle deserted. Wally and Flicker will have fled Lupine, and she'll have run before Biome gets here.

When we reach the wall, Hazel stops. "Kel, you test the boundary first. But, please, do it gently this time. If it's still up, come back to the castle. The rest of us will search for Willow and Soo-yeon. We're hoping the villains are going to tear themselves apart, but if not..."

Deadshot cracks her knuckles in the darkness. "Then it's my turn."

"If anyone else runs into Lupine or the others, run away. If they catch you, scream as loud as you can. We'll all come running, some of us at super-speed."

"I'm scared." Cammie's still clutching my hand.

"I don't even know why," Deadshot says indignantly. "You're the one who can go invisible and nobody even knows you're there. You can just hide if you want and—"

"Except I don't want to." Her voice is sharp. "I

never wanted to. I used my powers to *help* and it was because of me that—"

"Sorry," Deadshot says, and I'm still amazed by this new version of her. "I know you're the reason we're here. You're right. I'm scared too and I wish I could go invisible. So I'll have to be brave and hope we can do it together."

"Oh my god," Kel whispers really loudly. "Shottie is a secret soft."

"I hate you," Deadshot says.

"But what she really meant," Cammie whispers in my ear really close. "Was I love you."

I start giggling helplessly.

"What did you say, you little lizard? I heard you whispering. Effie, tell me what she said."

"Be nice, Shottie," Kel says. "We all like you better this way."

That completely takes the wind out of Deadshot's sails *of course* and I don't know if Kel did it on purpose or not.

"Are you all quite finished?" Hazel asks dryly. "I find it very hard to have faith when you're all bickering like this—or flirting, whichever it is. Sometimes it's hard to tell the difference."

"You're right." I smooth the laughter out of my voice. "We're ready to do the scary thing."

Everyone else chimes in their agreement too. It really is like being on a team.

"Okay. Let's go." Cammie pushes the button to open the secret door, and we all file out. The stairs are quiet and deserted.

Everyone looks at me, even Hazel. I want to look down, to stare at my feet and wait for the moment to pass. Instead, I clear my throat. "Okay. We're ready. Kel's going for the barrier. Cammie and I will find the way to the tower. Deadshot, Dopple and Hazel will hunt for Lupine."

Kel winks at us, and disappears down the stars as a rainbow blur. The rest of us rush after her. My heart's beating like I've been running for far longer.

The corridor to the throne room is deserted too. The doors at the end are wide open. It smells of smoke, and the furniture is a charred pile.

"Distraction, huh?" Deadshot grins. "No wonder I started to like you, Effie."

I glance down the eastern corridor where I got trapped by Wally and the wolves. This time I have to do better. I'll find Willow and Soo-yeon, and rescue the worst mutantsitting job ever.

"Good luck." I take a shaky breath.

"You too." Hazel draws both Dream and Nightmare, holding them across her chest. "See you when it's done." She strides off down the west corridor away from us. Deadshot's hot on her heels, juggling her handful of stones. Dopple creeps along at the rear.

"Guess I can't decide." Another Dopple stays with us. "Which way is more terrifying?"

"Let's find out." I clap him on the shoulder, and we follow Cammie east, scared of what we'll find there—victory, defeat, or something else entirely.

CHAPTER TWENTY-THREE

IN WHICH I MAKE A SERIES OF MISTAKES, RIGHT WHEN THINGS WERE SUPPOSED TO BE GETTING BETTER

IT DOESN'T TAKE LONG to reach the place where I was trapped. The suit of armour is piled in a mess against the wall. I pick up the helmet, wondering whether it'll help me, but it's so heavy that I drop it. The clang echoes all around. We all freeze.

"Oops." I bite my bottom lip. I've ruined the plan already.

Cammie shimmers, patterns of stone appearing all over her body.

Dopple groans. "I wish I was my duplicate right now."

We're frozen in place, but a whole minute ticks past, and there's still no sign of alarm.

"Let's all be much stealthier, okay?" Cammie whispers.

We creep further through the corridors, but every room we find is empty. Cammie was right. The plant kids aren't in this part of the castle. I'm getting more and more worried that Kel hasn't returned from the barrier yet. She could have made it there and back a bunch of times already. Maybe that just means she's gone back for Biome.

Through the castle windows, we can see the sun peeking over the horizon, painting the sky in faint streaks of colour. The whole world seems to be waiting for something, just like us. I really hope it's something good, and not another disaster. This time I manage to keep my mouth shut so I don't jinx it.

We finally reach a corridor with a series of archways. They lead onto a central courtyard of cobblestones with brown grass sticking up through them. On the other side, part of the castle wall has collapsed.

And rising in the distance is the obvious shape of—

"That's it," Cammie whispers. "The tower."

We jog across the courtyard and stand among the rubble. The tower must have risen very high once, and is still much taller than the rest of the castle. It looks like a tree sharpened into a pencil. The walls are wreathed in vines, with only the occasional glimpse of stone. The pointed turret is overrun with flowers, in a dazzling array of colours.

It's not that far away, although there's an outer stone wall in-between. Maybe we can climb it or—

"She'll kill us!" We freeze at the sound of Wally's voice nearby.

"That's what I'm telling you." Flicker's voice is cold and hard. "She's going to kill us *anyway*. We need to escape before she can."

"You can't even *think* that." Wally sounds as terrified as he did in his nightmare. I have a pang of sympathy. "She has eyes and ears—"

"Children." Lupine's voice is soft and honeyed. "You can't really be thinking of leaving my protection, can you? If you fly, you'll only run into the arms of Biome, and believe me, they will *not* be sympathetic."

"Keep away from us," Flicker says. "We won't let you hurt—"

Silence falls. Dopple and I exchange helpless glances. I don't know where Cammie has gone. Where are the others? Did Lupine attack them?

"Pick them up please, Deadshot," Lupine says. "Bring them to me."

I freeze. This can't be true. Deadshot can't really have gone over to the other side. Not after the change I saw in her. Could I have been fooled that easily? I suppose I've lied to people too, but I've never pretend to be someone's friend so utterly that—

"Kel, you too. Take the other."

"No," I gasp. There is *no way* Kel would turn on us, not even for Deadshot. I reach for Dopple's arm. "We need to get out of here. Something really bad is happening."

Kel and Deadshot walk around the corner. They're moving in a bizarre loping gait that reminds me of the wolves. They see us, and they smile identical smiles. Their teeth look very white in their mouths.

It's their eyes that terrify me. They're a lurid and intense green.

I remember that dream of Wally's. It was all true. Lupine can control people's minds.

"Are you surprised, children?" The words coming from Kel's mouth aren't hers. "Humans and mutants are animals too, little different to wolves."

Deadshot selects one stone from the collection in her palm. "Blam blam blam." The smile isn't hers. It's Lupine's.

The nightmare is unleashed on us, and there's no way I can wake up from it this time. I wish Hazel was here, to take me into that grey misty space between dreams. Except I'm stuck in real life, standing on the hard ground, feeling the morning chill.

The air shimmers, and Cammie becomes visible. "Get out of here, Effie. Find the kids."

Dopple grimaces, and there are now three of him in front of me. "Too many options, but we all agree on this."

The first stone leaves Deadshot's hand and hits one of the Dopples in the head. He collapses to the ground.

"Run," the other two shout.

"Please, Effie." Cammie turns her beautiful eyes on me. "Save the kids. Fix this."

There are so many things I want to say. I want to scream *why me* and tell them I'm not good enough for this. I'm only a baseline. But my friends are in danger, the plant kids are trapped, and everyone's relying on me. So I have to do this anyway.

I throw myself through the gap in the crumbling part of the castle wall, and run in a chaotic, zig-zag pattern across the ground. Something whines past my ear and there's a sharp cracking sound from the stones nearby. A sharp piece slices across my cheek. It stings, but nothing worse.

I'm waiting for Deadshot's next stone to hit me in the back and send me sprawling to the ground. A high-pitched cry comes from behind me. I don't know which one of my friends is hurt. I don't have time to stop and check.

All that's thrumming through my head is that I need to make the tower. When I hit the stone wall, I'm moving so fast it almost knocks all the breath from me. Everything hurts, but I hitch myself up and over. I sprawl onto my hands and knees. My breath comes in gasps. This is the worst case scenario but—

No. There's no time to get caught up in worrying.

I have to do this. Just like during the Dark Year, my family is depending on me. I get to my feet again, sprinting towards the tower. Running as if I'm still being chased, but maybe nobody cares. I have no powers, after all. There's no advantage to possessing me. That's all I've got going for me right now. I'm useless.

Surrounding the tower is a bunch of dead trees that might have been an orchard once. They're grey and spindly, nothing like the lush trees in Cybele's forest. These are skeletons, jabbing their weary bones into the grey sky. Rising tall from the middle of this graveyard of wood is the overgrown tower. It looks like it was once a prison, with someone trapped in the top of it, wishing their hair was long enough to reach the ground.

There's a single wooden door at the bottom, but it's

overgrown with a massive wall of thorns. Just like the tower, the thorns look like something out of a fairytale, built to a ridiculous scale. Each one is as thick as my arm, and longer than my body. Even if I had an enchanted axe from a fairytale, it would take me hours to hack my way through.

Why would Lupine imprison the children behind something like that?

I have no choice but to try, so I weave my way through the withered orchard anyway. Perhaps there's another door on the other side of the tower, or a rope of braided hair descending from the window.

As I get closer, the thorns retreat, as if they're scared.

By the time I reach the door, they've withered away, leaving my path clear.

Of course. Lupine didn't imprison them. Willow and Soo-yeon shut *themselves* in to be safe.

I put my hand on the door and turn the metal handle. It creaks open. Inside, it's surprisingly warm, as if the stone has been heated by the sun. It's very narrow, and a steep spiral staircase heads upwards, cut from rough stone.

"Effie!" A familiar and reassuring voice comes from behind me. "Wait! It's okay!"

I turn to see my sister striding across the ground. In front of her, wrapped in a spinning ball of water, is the figure of Lupine. She's struggling, but tendrils of water hold her arms and legs. It's definitely on the edge of what Airy's powers are capable of, and I wonder how much effort it takes to keep it aloft. Captured inside,

Lupine's face looks as ferocious and feral as her wolves.

There's no sign of my friends. Bad thoughts swirl in my head. All of them lying hurt. Worse than that. Deadshot's stones, fired like bullets. At least Lupine is caught now. I can relax. This is all over.

"Airy." My voice shakes. "Thank goodness you're here."

"Couldn't let you fight the villains alone, could I?" She laughs. "Turns out Wolf Lady doesn't do too well against a wall of water."

I sag against the open door of the tower. "I think the plant kids are here. Did you knock out Wally?"

"First thing I did." Her smile is wide and proud. "Kel's already off and running for Mutopia. Shouldn't be too long before the rescue party gets here. Might want to let the kids know, and we can meet them partway."

Relief floods through me so strongly I almost collapse to the ground. "Where are the others?"

"Recovering," Airy says. "They're all a bit shaken."

"Mind control. So freaky."

"You're telling me." Through one of the swirling gaps in the rings of water, I catch a glimpse of Airy's face.

Her eyes are a pure, stunning green.

Cold floods through me, and my stomach turns to liquid. "You're not my sister."

Airy laughs, and it's not hers anymore, but Lupine's instead. "Oh. And we were ever so close."

The rings of water come splashing to the ground,

making puddles. The wall of thorns begins to weave itself together again, but they're moving too slowly.

I close my eyes, feeling behind me. There's no way I can let her possess me. I'm the last chance. As soon as my hand touches the steps, I spin around and begin to climb.

"Is this your game?" Lupine's voice is mocking. "There's nowhere to go."

Nowhere except into the arms of the plant kids, who are scary and powerful. Except I've let the monster in with me.

It's time for another plan. Ignore the fact my *other* plans have turned into disaster. Ignore that Lupine has my sister in her thrall, and probably all my friends too.

Running is all I can do, so I carry on scrambling up the stairs.

The staircase is incredibly long. My lungs burn. My calves ache. My hands are scraped from the rough stone. And all the way, Lupine follows behind, her mocking voice calling. I tune it out.

There's always someone more powerful than me. It doesn't mean I can't beat them.

When I reach the top of the tower, I'm in a small circular room. A single arched window looks out, but from this angle, all I can see is sky. All that's in the room are two green-skinned children with messy, petal-strewn hair, staring at me with identical expressions.

Willow folds their arms across their chest. "Wow, Effie. You really messed this up."

"Yes." Soo-yeon looks at me with great disappoint-ment. "This is not how things were meant to go."

CHAPTER TWENTY-FOUR

AND IT ALL COMES DOWN TO THIS MOMENT! WHICH I AM MOSTLY UNPREPARED FOR

"I'M SO SORRY," I squawk. "Lupine fooled me with Airy and—"

"You're going to have to stop her," Willow says. "If she can control us, she can communicate directly with Cybele. That would be very, very bad."

"How bad?" I'm on the verge of freaking out.

"End of the world bad," Soo-yeon says.

"Potentially." Willow rolls their eyes. "You're so dramatic. You get that from Pear."

"Can't you get out of here? You know…" I flail my arms around loosely. "Do the vine thing."

"She's got us trapped in a forcefield, so we can't properly escape." Willow scowls at me, like I'm being far too slow for their liking. "And, like we keep telling you, if she gets control of us, we're talking—"

"End of the world." I take a deep breath. "Right. So get up on the roof. I'll stop her."

"Really." Soo-yeon arches their eyebrow at me. "How are you going to do that?"

"I'll tell her you went out the window."

"The truth." Willow nods seriously. "This is an amazing plan. Tell her where we are and—"

"I'll shove her out the window. She can't fly, can she?"

"No." Soo-yeon nudges their sibling. "I don't think she can fly, silly Willow. Maybe she can summon an army of crows or flying monkeys or—"

"Little baseline," Lupine's voice calls. She's close now. Too close.

"Stop mocking me and get out the window." I pretend I'm the Effie with the plan. The brave Effie. The one who stares at people in charge, who smiles and tells them lies. "Now."

"Oh what's at stake anyway?" Willow asks. "Only the fate of the world."

"I like relying on a human with no powers," Soo-yeon swings themself out the window. For a moment, they dangle there, grinning at me up-side down. "It has a certain dramatic flair."

Willow gives me a little finger wave and bounces up after their sibling. "Good luck, Finn Elizabeth. Don't let the world end! We'll have all our vines crossed for you!"

Then they're both gone.

I'm alone in the little tower room, waiting for a monster.

It only takes Lupine a minute to arrive. A smile crosses her face when she sees me. "I don't under-stand why you ran. You're only delaying the..." The smile vanishes, replaced by a frown so sharp I could cut myself on it. "And where have my sweet guests gone?"

"What guests?" I widen my eyes as wide as I can. Innocent, foolish Effie, stumbling around.

"Don't *bore* me. I have little patience for games."

"It's no game. The tower's empty. You can see that, right?"

One lip curls upwards at the corner, just like one of her wolves. "Would you like me to take over your mind, little creature? I could dangle you out the window until you tell me."

And there. She's given something away. She can't read my mind. Even if she can puppet my body around, she can't steal the one piece of knowledge she needs most. It's not that I *want* to be dangled out a window, but—

It's a weird thing to pop into your head.

The idea that you might die, and that you'll do it if you *have* to. Even if she drops me, and I plummet to the ground, I'll do it to protect the plant kids. It's better than the world ending.

Wow, that *is* very dramatic, isn't it? Soo-yeon would be proud.

It's not the first time I've been in a bad situation with someone threatening me. I remember standing in the street outside my grandmother's apartment. Three men with guns stood in a triangle around me. Four floors above, my Dads and my sister hid inside the walls. One man stepped forward and shoved the barrel of a gun hard against the back of my skull.

Sometimes I imagine that I can feel the indentation

of that gun even now. It's not true. There was a bruise, but it healed a long time ago. A circle inside a circle. The place where the bullet would have gone in. I wouldn't have felt a thing.

I would've let them pull the trigger that night to save my family. I said nothing, the truth of my family's hiding place locked behind my lips, while lies and tears fell instead. The man towered over me, while I collapsed on my knees. The gun felt like a drill, sending chips of bone flying as it pressed into my skull.

One of them kicked me in the stomach, so hard I curled up and retched until my throat stung. Another stood on my hand until two fingers broke, held there until the gene tester turned green and proved I was a baseline. One spat on me, and then they walked away.

I'm in a situation like this again. I'm the one who can save the people I love.

I can do this again.

"Talk to me, Finn Elizabeth." Lupine grins wider. "Tell me where those little brats of Biome's are hiding. Save your skin. Save your *friends*."

My eyes move up until I'm holding Lupine's green gaze. "I don't know what you're talking about. The kids were already gone. They've got weird powers. You know this."

"Stubborn child." She reaches out and tips my chin up. "Look into my eyes."

For a moment, I think about telling her they escaped out the window. I don't think it'll help. She'll use me to manipulate the plant kids, threaten them with watching my death if they don't capitulate. I don't want them to have to make that choice. I'll make it on my own.

I blink, and I smile, and I stare into the pure green pools of her eyes.

Let me drown in them. She'll get nothing from my corpse.

Strangely, it doesn't *feel* like anything to have your brain taken over. One moment, it's only my voice in my head, the old familiar one that rattles around in there and narrates my life and wonders so many things, both deep and deeply silly.

And then someone else is in there too. Another deafening voice, booming and echoing around the rooms inside my head.

"Mind control." Lupine uses my lips to say it. "This is why they wouldn't let me onto their precious island. Those freakish monsters with their flowery words looked me up and down and said *no*. Can you believe that?"

"Of course I can," I say, and Lupine doesn't bother to stop my lips. Maybe she wants me to talk in the hope I'll give her information. "You can't use people as puppets."

She lifts my arms up above my head. They're stiff and awkward. It feels as if I'm being posed like an action figure. I spin clumsily around in a full circle until we're face to face again.

Lupine glares at me. "But that's exactly what I'm doing. It may contradict their rules, but I'm only using what nature has bestowed on me. Their precious Cybele blessed me with this power."

"I don't think so." She clamps my jaw shut, but I keep talking through my clenched teeth. "Not all powers come from the earth."

"It doesn't matter." She gestures and I spin towards the window, unsteady on my feet. "Biome's unnatural children will reveal themselves to me, or else you shall dive to your death. Then I'll move onto your sister, and your friends one after the other. Eventually, they'll slink out of their forest hole and submit to me."

"What do you want them for?"

"I shall put my hand around Cybele's throat and squeeze until she gives me a place of my own to lay my head. I won't give up my power for a spot on Biome's precious island, and I won't slink from place to place, trying to pass for human. She can build me my own island, for my animals and I, and anyone who wishes freedom from Mutopia's own mind control."

"There's no mind control on Mutopia," I tell her.

"Isn't there? Can I call your sister a boy? Can I call you a baseline or request your Chatterbox conform to their birth sex? It's a control of *ideas*, but control all the same."

I imagine what my Dads would say if they were here, or Airy. They don't need to be. I can speak for myself.

"It's called basic decency."

"Yet they enforce it, which shows it's not so basic after all." She smirks at me, as if this is a victory.

"To make a place that's safe for everyone. How does it hurt *you* to call Airy a girl?"

"It forces me to confirm to your shared fantasy of—
"

I force myself to move towards the window. Her control on my body is loose, like my limbs dangle in her hands. It gives me some freedom, but then her mind clenches tightly and my body comes to a halt.

"What are you doing?" Her voice stabs into my head and makes it ache.

"I don't want to listen to you." I wrench my mouth up into something that approximates a smile, fighting her the whole way.

"You're braver than you look." Lupine grins savagely at me, far fiercer than her wolves. "Yet I don't believe you."

"I made my peace with dying for my family a long time ago."

"You're only a child." Her lip curls.

"The Dark Year didn't care about that."

She laughs. "You're human. You know nothing about the Dark Year."

I don't tell her my secrets. She doesn't deserve them. Lying head to toe inside the narrow space of the wall, sharing breath and warmth. Palming medicine and hiding it in an oversized coat, under cover of buying groceries. Looking into the eyes of people who would kill me the second they knew who I harboured in my home. Mutants were one thing, mutant sympathisers were far worse. Regardless of my age, the punishment would have been severe. Even now, my mind flinches away from the stories I heard.

Even then, I hated that these people with guns

could bully people. They could build a world filled with enough fear that even my fathers hid themselves away. My small acts of rebellion, to steal and to stand, seemed so small, but the shadows they cast were large.

Large enough to keep my family safe.

I'll stand here too. If I do it for long enough, perhaps I can distract her, or buy time for someone with actual superpowers to fight back. All I have is my stubbornness and the memory of a gun barrel pressed to the back of my head.

Speaking of guns, perhaps there is one thing I can do.

I resist her power as much as I can, taking tiny shuffling steps backwards.

"Are you really going to fight me like this? I'll find those saplings eventually. Your sacrifice is worth nothing."

I grit my teeth, and raise my hand, inch by painful inch. There's pressure inside my head as she clamps down on my muscles. I fight her all the way. I curl my fingers so I'm pointing at her, like an accusation.

"It's always worth fighting," I say.

"Ridiculous child." Her eyes dance, an impossible green. "Very well. See how far fighting gets you."

Her control is gone. My head sings rather than throbs. I've still got my hand outstretched.

The first notes that escape my throat are hoarse and hesitant. They sound like something plunked out on an out-of-tune piano in a forgotten room in a rambling old house. My voice catches on a sob, and steadies itself.

The next notes are pure and true, ringing clear through the stone room, the echoes buoying them even higher.

"What is this?" Lupine laughs. "The Mutopian national anthem?"

I reach the crescendo of the melody, and dip down to begin it again. This time, the notes come out slightly rasping, crisp at the edges, but perfect.

Something solid presses against my hand, taking shape in the curl of my palm. My index finger presses against something warm and humming.

Dream.

CHAPTER TWENTY-FIVE

IN WHICH A LOT OF THINGS HAPPEN VERY FAST, AND WE FIND AN END TO THE STORY AFTER ALL

"WHAT IS THAT?" Lupine's eyes widen, drenching us both in emerald.

"Blam," I say.

I feel her mind *reach* for me, that voice beginning to speak inside my head. A single, commanding syllable, but on her indrawn breath there's a single heartbeat of freedom.

Enough time to pull the trigger.

Dream is so heavy in my grip. I'm not sure what it's made of, but it's warm and soft. The barrel sings, completing the melody in a triumphant note. Pink and hazy light erupts from the gun, shot through with gold.

The light wreathes Lupine's face like a spinning, delirious halo. Her mind clamps around me, one last reflexive movement. It sends me staggering backwards with hurried steps, fast and jerky like I'm being pushed.

Lupine's eyes dim, that unreal green shading back to something ordinary. Her control is gone, the tight feeling in my skull evaporating. The nagging voice of her powers is silent.

Except I'm still moving, and I bump against the lip of the window. Dream dissolves in my hand. I'm holding nothing. Momentum has hold of me.

I tip backwards. My arms both flail outwards, but I only catch air.

After all this, my rebellion, my impossible summoning of Dream, my defeat of Lupine, and I'm going to tumble out the window to my death anyway.

I can't make sense of the world from upside down.

Wind rushes past my face. The landscape blurs. There is blue and green and grey, but they're abstract swirls.

I'm falling to my death. My life doesn't flash in front of my eyes. All I can catch onto is a few thoughts. At least I defeated the villain, saved my sister, and my friends. There are worse ways to go. All these borrowed hours since that moment in the street outside the apartment building when I thought I was going to die.

And then something *jerks* on me. I'm not falling anymore, or I'm falling *differently*. This is how I imagine it feels to be a monkey, flying from tree to tree. Soo-yeon moves through the air beside me, one vine hand wrapped around my wrist. Their touch is cool, and I smell something fresh and faintly spicy.

Willow takes hold of my other side, and together we all swing in a wide arc, like this is an enormously joyful experience for both of them. They land lightly on the ground, with me tangled between them.

I'm still catching up on the fact that I'm somehow alive, but the first thing I think of is—

"Lupine!" My voice croaks. "What's she doing?"

"Currently under the influence of Dream," Willow says. "That was *very* clever, summoning the gun like that. Wolf Lady be out for a bit. One of us should put a sack over her head."

I blush. "I wasn't sure if it would work."

"Effie," someone screams in the distance.

"Oh, here comes the brave rescue," Soo-yeon says. "They would've been just in time to watch you go splat. Lucky we intervened."

I don't care that they would have been late. Here are my friends.

Kel reaches me first, rainbows dancing around her shoes. She's got so much momentum that I go falling backwards for the second time in a handful of minutes, but this time it's much less distance to the ground. Deadshot throws herself into the pile and almost knocks the breath out of me, and then I can't even tell who's next because there are too many people smothering me.

After a few minutes, we all get to our feet and everyone has their turn hugging everyone else and explaining their breathless part in the battle. I have to tell my part over and over again. Cammie hasn't let go of my hand the entire time, and I don't want her to. Even Deadshot seems impressed.

"Does that mean you've got a mutant power?" Her eyes are wide. "You summoned Dream!"

Hazel is beaming at me, like I achieved something

amazing. "Dream has a life of her own. She chose to go to Effie in response to the song. Probably because she likes them."

"Everyone likes Effie," Cammie says in such warm tones I feel my cheeks might combust.

I'm trying to line up words on my tongue to say them, something inspiring and maybe flirtatious. Can I do that? All my carefully ordered words are knocked from my head by an enormous crash.

Someone screams. It might be me. Past my friends, an enormous woman with stone skin rips the top off the tower. I almost collapse to my knees. This is totally unfair! Some ferocious giant sent to crush us, just when we think we've won.

"Auntie Lys!" The plant kids tear off in the direction of the tower, flowers springing up in their wake. "Wait for us!"

"Oh." My voice shakes. "Ms. Sefo."

"Not only her." Deadshot stares as something dark and spider-like flickers through air like black lightning, zig-zagging towards the castle.

"Penance," Kel whispers. "The scariest one. She'll deal with Lupine."

"We have bigger problems." Deadshot grabs hold of us, and I think it's an excuse to touch Kel.

Then I notice who's walking in our direction.

"Quick," Kel gasps. "We need to come up with a story."

We're staring at two tall green figures. A samurai sword and a baseball bat whirl around their heads.

They're holding huge, spiked clubs that seem like they could swat any of us really, really easily.

"Monsters," I gurgle, even though I know exactly who they are. It's Chatterbox and Marvellous, come to get their kids back. Who aren't even *here* right now because they're gone to meet one of their scary aunts.

We're the ones who went running off without any word. While looking after their children. Only to get captured by mutants. This is not a good advertisement for our services. At all.

"Oh yikes," Dopple says in a tiny voice. "We're really in trouble." There's only one of him, frozen in place next to the rest of us. Only one decision to make here. Running wouldn't help.

As Biome makes their way towards us, the clubs shrink down until only simple daggers remain. These are the weapons Dad Adé was making for them. The wood from the crown of the forest is very powerful.

Chatterbox and Marvellous come to a halt. Cammie tries to hide behind me. *Now* there are four Dopples, all ready to flee in different directions. Deadshot is staring at the ground. A faint rainbow ripples around Kel, a sure sign of imminent flight.

"The Mutantsitters Club." Chatterbox's voice is flat.

"You've had an interesting time." Marvellous stares at all of us, dagger in her hand.

I don't really think they're going to *hurt* us, but the disappointment of the Founders and actual amazing superheroes feels almost as bad. This is all my fault. I need to take responsibility.

I step forward, right up to them. "We're really

sorry." I meet their gaze. "But we did our best, and tried to make the best of a bad situation."

Chatterbox's eyes go wide. "I was going to apologise to *you*. For having to save our ridiculous children who roamed off to tame a pair of wolves?"

"Oh." I blink, feeling like my brain is about to trip over itself. "Um. Well, I'm glad we could, you know, save the day."

"Lupine is one of the most deadly mutants in existence," Marvellous says.

"Not any more." Chatterbox's gaze goes to where Penance and Ms. Sefo are coming towards us, Lupine cradled inside a cage of blades. "Thanks to you. I've always had a soft spot for plucky underdogs. Nice job, Effie."

I don't know how they know what happened, but the actual Chatterbox being *proud* of me is going to take a while to get used to.

"Mum! Pear!" Willow and Soo-yeon are perched on Moodring's shoulders, seemingly unfazed by the entire adventure.

"You both sound far too happy," Marvellous observes.

"You should have seen it," Willow says. "Effie saved the day all by themself. They fought Lupine's mind control and threatened to throw themself out the window! And then they shot her with Dream and accidentally fell."

"But we saved them from going splat," Soo-yeon says. "Which you should factor into any punishment you're planning."

Petals cascade down around Willow's head. "We also hid in that tower and barred the way, so she couldn't control us. Really, we should get almost as much praise as Effie, if you think about it."

Marvellous shakes her head. "You were doing well up until that last part."

"Pushed it too far," Soo-yeon says with some scorn.

"Worth a try," Willow shrugs.

"Come here, you ridiculous children," Dylan says, and the two of them throw themselves at their parents, where they all tangle their vines together and in moments they're all covered with a riot of orange, red and yellow flowers.

"Those kids are a handful," Alyse tells me. "I told Dylan and Dani that you'd do your best. We've been hunting, but we couldn't detect them up until a few minutes ago."

"That's when I knocked out forcefield boy," Dead-shot says.

"What happened to him and Flicker?" I ask. "They were controlled too, you know."

"They'll be coming back with us," Ms. Sefo says. "We'll try and integrate them into Mutopia. At least give them a chance."

"They're already on their last chance." Feral stalks up to us, fur all sticking out. Wally and Flicker walk ahead of her, looking extremely downcast. "If this one here shocks me one more time, the claws will come out."

"Do what Feral says," I tell them. "And you can come home with us."

"Why would we want to do that?" Flicker sneers.

Wally elbows her in the side. "Shut *up*. It's got to be better than running around doing what Lupine wants all the time. We might even have friends."

Flicker rolls her eyes, but doesn't have any real argument.

"Right." Chatterbox has finally disentangled themself from their family. "Let's get back to the island, and we can talk about rewards and punishments."

I'm pretty sure we're getting rewards after what they said, but I'm still a little nervous. We head away from the castle, down the overgrown path that snakes down to the main road. I'm at the back of the line.

"Here." Kel sidles up to me and holds out a chunk of rock.

"What's this?"

"The thing. You know. The Deadshot thing."

I grin triumphantly. "You *do* like her."

Kel makes an exaggerated sad face. "I don't know *why*, but yes."

"She's not so bad," I say. "When you get to know her. Occasionally sweet, even."

"I've seen no evidence of it. Maybe you *should* hit me."

I heft the rock in my hand and press it lightly to her temple. "There you go. Cured of Deadshot."

Kel looks up ahead, to where Deadshot keeps looking over her shoulder. "It didn't take. I still feel all fizzy and dizzy when I look at her. Like when I've just started running, and the whole world is light and airy under me."

"You've got it bad," I say with a gurgle of laughter.

"Shut up. You're way worse."

Up ahead, Cammie is walking alongside Dopple. I watch the sway of her hair and the way she gives a half-smile and covers it with her hand. I'm about to protest, to say that I don't feel that way, but Kel's been honest with me about something *way* more embarrassing.

"I almost asked her to kiss me."

"Gross." Kel's nose wrinkles. "Why would you do that?"

"You want to kiss Deadshot!"

"I do not!"

"You do so!"

"I hate this conversation," Kel says. "I'll race you home."

"Last one home has to kiss Deadshot. Or gets to, depending on your point of view."

She hits me in the shoulder. "You're very annoying, Effie. Have I ever told you that?"

We've been walking past a couple of small trees on the side of the road, and they suddenly sprout heads.

"So Kel likes Deadshot," Willow says loudly, but nobody turns around.

"And Effie likes Cammie," Soo-yeon chimes in.

"Shut up," I hiss.

The two kids look at us with identical smiles. "What's in it for us?"

Kel and I both stop dead, looking at them in horror. "What can you possibly want?"

The twins trade glances, their vines tangling together.

"Regular babysitting time," Willow says. "Once a week."

Soo-yeon nods. "We promise not to escape the island. But you *do* need to take us on adventures."

"This is blackmail," I splutter.

"Wow, they know what that is." Willow says to their sibling with an eye-roll, and then turns back to me. "How about it?"

I catch Kel's eye. It's not the *worst* idea in the world. Surely next time we babysit the plant kids, it can't possibly go this badly.

"Fine," I say. "The Mutantsitters Club lives on."

"Good decision." Willow smirks.

Then the plant kids swing themselves over and perch on our shoulders, and we follow the others down the path back home.

ACKNOWLEDGMENTS

So many people to thank again!

To Amanda, Hsinju, Logan, and Shana: thank you so much for helping me strike the right tone and tell the right story.

To my family: thank you for supporting me when I spend way too much time writing, thinking about writing, and getting emotional about writing.

To Ash and Christina: thank you for reading, and for being amazing inspirations as MG writers.

To my writing support network: thank you always to the feral raccoons in Team Trash (Andy, Crystal, Leah, Mallory, Melo, Michelle, Monica, Nat, Nina, SinJ, and SoftJ) who are always there to boost me and back me. And of course to Rosa, Shannon, Mary, Charlotte, and E.M who are always so supportive through everything. I couldn't do this without all of you. And of course, thanks to the many, many people who've read, supported, and boosted my work. Self publishing is a strange and lonely journey sometimes, but all of you have made an enormous difference in making this series—as well as this book—a reality.

ABOUT THE AUTHOR

SJ Whitby is an author. That's about all you need to know, really. They're nonbinary, just like Effie, and they live in New Zealand. It's also an island (or three islands), but it's far less interesting than Mutopia. They also write the Cute Mutants series for older teenagers and adults.

twitter.com/sjwhitbywrites

instagram.com/sjwhitbywrites

patreon.com/sjwhitby

www.ingramcontent.com/pod-product-compliance
Lightning Source LLC
Chambersburg PA
CBHW030932210726

48290CB00007B/2165